# Jackson Hole
## Uneasy Eden

# Jackson Hole
## Uneasy Eden

## Fiction by
# Warren Adler

HOMESTEAD PUBLISHING
Moose, Wyoming

ISBN 0-943972-62-0 (hardcover)

*Library of Congress Cataloging-in-Publication Data*
Adler, Warren.
Jackson Hole, Uneasy Eden : fiction / by Warren Adler. — 1st ed.
p.    cm.
ISBN 0-943972-62-0 (hard : alk. paper)
I. Title.
PS3551.D64J33  1997
813'.54—dc21                                              97-8825
                                                            CIP

First Edition
Printed in the United States of America
on recycled, acid free paper.

1  3  5  7  9  10  8  6  4  2

Published by
HOMESTEAD PUBLISHING
Box 193 • Moose, Wyoming 83012

*Dedicated to Mary Hansen Mead Steinhour*

I t was our last day at the Masa Mara game park in Kenya. My wife Sunny and I had been on safari in Africa for ten days and were heading back by chartered plane to Nairobi, where we would rest overnight at the Norfolk Hotel before flying back to the States in the morning.

Our outfitter requested that we take a "hitchhiker" from another safari whose camp had been rained out. We agreed, and it was my luck to be seated next to this person who, as you might have guessed, was Mary. When we were airborne, I looked out of the window at the high plain below with the magnificent Mount Kilimanjaro dominating the horizon.

"If only I could find a place of such beauty in the States," I sighed.

"I guess you've never been to Jackson Hole?" Mary said.

"No," I replied. "Have you?"

"I am Jackson Hole," she said, or might have said. More

than eight years have elapsed since that moment, and perhaps the story has been embellished by the telling and retelling. But the fact is that four months later, we were with Mary in Jackson Hole. It was the weekend of our anniversary, which might have contributed to our instant love affair with this magnificent valley.

"This is the place," my wife said to me as we viewed the Tetons that weekend from the porch of our cabin at Spring Creek Resort. I agreed emphatically.

We saw Mary many times as we journeyed enthusiastically from visitor, to renter, to home builder. We attended the weddings of two of her children and were pleased to meet and befriend her lovely parents, Cliff and Martha Hansen. Cliff had been a respected governor and senator from Wyoming and is much revered, deservedly so, in this state. We eagerly supported Mary when she ran for governor and were disappointed when she lost.

We were delighted when Mary met Dick Steinhour, fell in love, and eventually married. We reveled in her newfound happiness. The news of her untimely death went through us like a hot spear.

Meeting Mary that day in Africa changed our lives profoundly. It was she who gave us the gift of this valley and it is to her that we will be eternally grateful.

And despite her physical loss to us, she has left us with a snapshot of herself that is engraved in our minds and forever will be the door through which our memories of her enter.

It is early morning, the sun flickering through the mist. A horse emerges from the mist, revealing a rider, sunbeams playing on her yellow slicker, catching the sparkle in her blue eyes, her lips forming a radiant smile. She is pushing her cattle along Spring Gulch Road, a picture of the quintessential cowboy forever free in heart and spirit. She waves. We wave back.

For us, that figure is the timeless image of our beautiful valley and its people. Thank you, Mary.

Warren Adler
*Jackson Hole*
*January 5, 1997*

# CONTENTS

# Jackson Hole
## Uneasy Eden

# 1
## THE PROMISE

Steadman could hear the tires crackling over the gravel as it cut in from Spring Gulch Road and moved west toward the Circle Bar S ranch house. Thirty years ago, he had sited the house on high ground overlooking the Snake River so that, through the west-facing windows, they could see the jagged peaks of the Tetons, glimmering silvery in the morning light. From the east windows they could see the forest of lodgepoles that gave them the feel of complete privacy. Farther east, beyond the lodgepoles, had been the pastures for cattle.

Now what was that boy's name again? he asked himself as he waited, wondering why he had even consented to see him. Steadman had received offers to buy the ranch before, but he had turned them all down. Actually, it wasn't a working ranch any longer, not since Amy had died and he had sold off his herd.

Without Amy, gone two years now, ranching made no sense anymore. They had been partners in the working aspect of the ranch, a cow and calf operation that made just enough to keep them going from year to year. All in all, it was a hard but happy life, and they both loved it.

They had been married for fifty years and had no children; their family was the ranch hands, and their children were the calves that they helped birth and baby each year, worrying about their health just like any loving parents would. Life was rhythmical and predictable, almost, depending on the weather. The ranching way of life suited them, and if there were hardships, they got through them with cheerful resolve.

Steadman had grown up on the ranch. His father had bought it from the original homesteaders, and when he brought Amy here from Casper—where he had met her at a rodeo—she fell in love with it, every rock and tree, every piece of dirt and sage, every cow and calf and horse. Most of all, she loved the ever-hovering mountains, never tiring of the play of light that made them look different from moment to moment, day or night.

They had designed their bedroom and placed their bed so that the first thing they saw in the morning, when the weather was clear, of course, was the jagged peaks of the range. It was like a morning light show and never failed to thrill them.

"There they are," Amy would say, her first words when she opened her eyes from sleep. "Means we're still alive, Aubrey."

Not having children was a bitter disappointment for both of them. But the power of their love for each other weathered that storm, just as it weathered whatever blows destiny dealt them. But they did believe that life balanced out and that they were lucky to have the gift of this piece of earth in Jackson Hole. They felt certain that they lived in the most beautiful and magical valley on the planet.

The problem was, as Steadman saw it now, that this beautiful fifty-mile-long and twelve-mile-wide valley that stretched from Yellowstone to the Hoback had been discovered by the world. In his mind, the world meant "trespassers", aliens who had no appreciation for the glory and sanctity of this place and whose only motive was material gain.

The evidence was all around him. Land that once had sold for $50 to $100 an acre now was running into the thousands. Commerce had arrived in the form of stockbrokers, chain stores, fast-food operators, fancy restaurants. Big houses were mushrooming everywhere. Whereas he and Amy once knew everybody in Jackson Hole, he was seeing more and more strange faces. Change appeared to be accelerating quite rapidly.

Not that life in the valley had ever been totally static. There had always been dude ranches attracting folks who craved a Western experience, and the old moneyed families had bought up large tracts for their own recreation, but there remained a sense that the land was sacred, not to be sacrificed on the altar of commercialism. It was different now. The tourists and the developers had invaded the land, and the operative word was "profit". Steadman and the other old locals used another word to describe what was happening. Greed!

"Don't let them do it to the Circle Bar S, Aubrey," Amy whispered with her dying breath. If the situation were reversed, he would have asked her to pledge to the same wish.

"No way, my love," Steadman vowed. "No way."

Many of his ranching friends were selling out to the

developers. Selling out was the only sensible way that they could liquidate and provide for their heirs. It was a sorry situation.

Inevitably, he knew, he would have to sell the ranch before he died. Dying without heirs would put the land at risk; it might be auctioned off to the highest bidder to do with as they wished, without restraint. Steadman was determined to pass it on to someone who would respect it, create a home here and not develop it as a subdivision. In Steadman's mind, subdividing would be destroying its integrity. To him, money was very low on his list of priorities. Besides, he had promised Amy.

Since Amy died—even during her funeral—he had been turning down offers for the ranch on what was almost a weekly basis. Most of them came from real-estate people. He could almost smell the stench of greed before they turned onto the ranch road. They would bring their big smiles and sincere looks, promising the moon, not realizing that he was sizing them up at first glance and rejecting whatever baloney they were selling outright. He hardly listened to their blatant pitches and promises of riches, although he showed them the same hospitality that Amy would have provided to anyone who crossed their threshold.

What annoyed him most was his own loss of trust. Once, he had trusted people. Locals had always lived by the ethic of honesty and straight-talk. People said what they believed to be the truth. A man's word was sacrosanct, and a handshake was more binding than words on paper. Steadman believed that knowing how it once had been gave him a special insight into people and their real motives.

Yet he had never given up hope that one day someone would arrive to whom he could safely turn over the stewardship of his land, someone who would revere and respect its character, someone who would make it his home and not a profit center.

But when someone came with an offer and a basketful of promises, he was always wary and on his guard. He imagined he could sense who would be likely to put another nail in the valley's coffin. So far, a steady stream of that kind had beat a path to his door. He considered them the enemy, the people who were hell-bent on ruining his beloved valley by chopping it into pieces, devouring it like vultures over carrion.

"Thanks for seeing me," the man said. Steadman took him for early fifties, lean, athletic, strong chin, blue-eyes, steel gray hair, serious. No big smile, which was a plus.

"Care for a drink?" Steadman asked. He had set out a pitcher of iced tea, lemon and mugs.

"That iced tea would be fine," the man said. His name, Steadman remembered, was Everett Carter. He was from New York, he had told him on the telephone. Saw his ranch from the air. Liked the setting. Any chance of talking business?

Steadman had liked his voice and his straightforward approach. Why not? He had already said "no" in his mind. Besides, without Amy, life was lonely and people to talk to were rare. Sometimes he was so lonely he would not have turned down a dialogue with the devil.

Steadman poured the man a mug of iced tea and pointed to a chair across from his own. Carter took the mug, sipped, then looked around him, his glance settling on the view of the Tetons.

"Great view," he said, putting Steadman on his guard. He was particularly wary of compliments. This one, however, came without a smile. Steadman merely nodded acknowledgment.

"What do you do in New York?" Steadman asked.

"Investment banker," Carter replied.

"Made a lot of money in the last few years?"

"That I did," Carter said. "Not ashamed of it, either. My father drove a delivery truck for a bakery. Never made much. I guess I figured I evened things out for him."

"You say you're lookin' for land?"

"Not just land. I'm looking for home. I'm planning on leaving New York."

"For good?"

"Why not?" Carter said, drinking another deep draught of his iced tea. "Been through here as a kid. I've always dreamed of a home here."

"Want to run cows, be a cowboy?"

"Sorry. No interest. I'm not coming here to do business, Mr. Steadman. Besides, I don't want the hassle."

"It's a hassle. More so these days. Hard going."

"What I'm looking for is a spread near the river with lots of land, a great view, a place for the kids to come. Maybe keep some horses."

"Got kids, have you?"

"Two. They're grown. One in college. One getting married. I want a place for my grandkids to appreciate and enjoy. Teach them the values of the West. Maybe I'm jumping the gun but that's what I'd like to happen."

"We never had kids," Steadman said, sipping his iced tea. He was sizing up the man, his opinion wavering, but he was not rejecting the man outright.

"Where'd you get the idea I want to sell out?" Steadman asked.

"I told you. I just took a shot," Carter said. "I believe in going after things face to face. If you're not interested, then I'll just be getting on. There's no harm in asking."

"You learned that in the investment banking business?"

"I learned that in life, Mr. Steadman. You want something. You go for it."

"No real-estate people in the bushes?"

"I like to deal direct."

Steadman continued to size up the man. He admitted to liking the man's look. His attitude, too.

"What would you do with this land?"

"Do?" Carter frowned and cocked his head. He seemed confused. Steadman refused to explain himself, watching Carter as he framed an answer. "I told you, Mr. Steadman. I'm looking for a home. That's it."

"You retiring?"

"Hell no. But I have left the firm. I've got lots of interests. And today we hook up with computers and faxes. You can be anywhere."

"Still want to make more money?"

"I'm in the keeper stage. I just want to keep what I got. Live here and keep what I made."

"Got plenty, do you?"

"A lot more than I need. As we say in the trade, I've hit my number."

"What number was it?" Aubrey asked.

"More than enough," Carter said, smiling for the first time.

Steadman shrugged, but didn't pry any further. A man who knew when he had enough was a smart man, he thought, warming to Carter.

"This valley is a way of life for most of us been here a long spell. Was a time we couldn't get green vegetables but once a week. Had one movie screen. Knew everybody in town." Now I'm talking like one of those old damned fools, Steadman thought, stopping himself. Amy would have shut him up fast.

"Must have been wonderful living here in the old days," Carter said.

"It sure was," Steadman agreed, forcing himself to crowd out the memories. The fact was that all his waking thoughts lately were about the past. He grew silent for a long moment, his eyes wandering to the mountains. Still here after a 100 million years, he thought. Saw a lot of us come and go. One day he'd go, too. Problem was he didn't know when. Nobody could predict when their time was over.

Suddenly he thought of the future as an affliction. What would he do without this land? Probably rent a small place in town and head for the desert in Arizona or Utah. Winters in Jackson were rough on old bones.

He might do some traveling. See the world he had missed during those years of ranching. After all, by any standard, the sale of the ranch would bring more than enough to live on for the rest of his life. He and Amy hardly ever traveled. Once they had taken a package tour of France and Germany. Another time they went to Mexico. They had derived some mild enjoyment on the tours but couldn't wait to get home.

"So you just took a shot?" Steadman asked.

"It's the way I operate," Carter replied.

Steadman rubbed his chin, still sizing up the man, but fast reaching a conclusion as to the man's motives and character.

"The point is, Mr. Steadman, are you in a selling mood or not?"

"Could be," Steadman said. "With Amy gone . . . my wife. She died two years ago. Without her . . . well, I just sold off the herd. Too hard for a man of seventy-five." Steadman became pensive, then looked into Carter's eyes. "To the right man, I might be willing to sell out."

"So my shot found its mark," Carter said, chuckling amiably. "Goes to show. You don't ask. You don't get the order. Apparently then, you'll entertain an offer."

"Depends."

"On what?"

"I need a rock solid unbreakable promise that this land stays intact. No development. No chopping it. It stays the Circle Bar S, just like it sits now. Get my drift?"

"Why would I want to chop it up?" Carter asked.

"Money."

"I told you about that. I hit my number. I don't need any more money. As for the name, its got history and character. Why change it?" He leveled his eyes directly into Steadman's. "I'm prepared to make you an offer you can't refuse."

"Yes I can, Carter. It's your promise I need more than the money."

"I get the picture. No development. I'll put it in writing if you want."

Aubrey had given that matter lots of thought. Could he trust a piece of paper? Contracts were made to be broken. Deed restrictions could be ignored. Legal challenges launched. The valley was getting too damned litigious, another sign of a society going to pot. Smart lawyers could do anything nowadays.

Integrity was what he was looking for. There was another dimension to this, Aubrey knew. He had been brought up to believe in the sanctity of property rights. It was a valley tradition that a man had a right to do what he wished with his property as long as he was sensitive to his neighbor's rights and needs. The standard was fairness and common sense, which was embedded more in a man's character than in the rule of law.

"If it was just the money, it would be easy," Steadman said.

"I know what you're thinking, Mr. Steadman," Carter said. He took a deep sip of his iced tea, and Steadman refilled his mug from the pitcher. "You think I'm one of those sharp guys from New York on the prowl for a deal that stacks the deck for himself. And you don't know me from Adam. You don't know my history or my reputation. Hell, to you, I'm just a fellow that dropped from the sky."

"You got that right, Carter," Steadman said. The man had indeed read his thoughts.

"There's no way I can reassure you. As I said, I'd be glad to put it in writing, but I'll bet you don't trust that either. You're going to have to lead with your gut here, Mr. Steadman. You're going to have to judge me by instinct. Oh, I'll give you more than a fair price. You know that. I'll pay a premium for this spot and you know that, too. And the reason I'll pay a premium is because this a fabulous place for me and my family to put down stakes, call home. Just me and my family. Hell, I'll probably be joining up with the folks, like yourself, who want to keep unchecked development out of the valley."

"A good speech, Carter," Steadman said. "But it'll still be a gamble on my part."

"Yes it will," Carter agreed.

"You're probably thinking I'm a damned fool. Take the money and run, you're probably thinking."

"Not at all. I can plainly see that money is not the issue here. What I'm thinking is how I can assure you that I intend no development, that I'd be buying this place for me and my family. I'll be glad to provide you with any references you might want, anything that might help mold your judgment of me. It's your call."

Steadman contemplated the man's face and bearing, looking for the answer to that question. He poured more iced tea and took a light sip.

"Afraid so, Carter."

"But I won't make my offer until you give me a firm commitment as to your intent. Fair enough?"

"Fair enough," Steadman agreed.

Carter slapped his thigh, rose and put his iced-tea mug on the table beside Steadman.

"I'm staying at the Spring Creek Resort for a few days. You think it over and you decide. All I can say is that I give you my solemn promise that I'll meet your conditions whether you want it in writing or you'll take my word for it. Believe me, I understand how important such a commitment is to you, and I'm prepared to honor it."

Steadman stood up, and the men shook hands. He imagined he could sense the man's integrity through the touch of his flesh. Then the man turned, went back to his car, and drove through the trees. Steadman could hear the fading sound of the tires crackling away on the gravel.

He stepped off the porch and walked along the river dike for awhile, then headed back through the lodgepoles into the pastureland. Lack of irrigation had killed the grass. Now the sage was taking over, getting back its rights to the land. The sage, after all, was there first and was returning to its rightful habitat.

Steadman walked along the gravel road, then headed north beside the now-empty irrigation ditches that fed the grass and the cows along which he and Amy and the hands had pushed the cattle to new growth, then up to the mountains for grazing. It was a good life, and it was over.

As he walked along the barbed-wire fences that still marked the bounds of the ranch, he thought about the man.

Was this the person who would fulfill the promise he had made to Amy? He had liked the way the man put it: 'I hit my number.' It suggested to him that man's greed was finite, that the thirst for more finally could be tamed and harnessed.

"Is this the right man to turn the land over to?" he asked aloud as he headed back to the barren loneliness of the ranch house, hoping that, somehow, his plea would reach Amy and she would respond with some sign.

The walk, which he once could do in minutes, took far longer than it ever had before, and when he reached the porch again he was winded and tired and had shooting pains in his thighs and back. Old age was arriving, and there was no mistaking its onset. It was time, he decided. The old way of life was dead.

That night, he continued to wrestle with the problem. He always had prided himself on his judgment of other men's motives. Wyoming people, he believed, had a sixth sense about people. Was this the man? He wished Amy were here to help him make this decision. She always was better at judging people. She could tell the good from the bad, the innocent from the guilty, the selfless from the greedy.

He hardly slept, and when he awoke he was more tired than he was before he went to bed. After a light breakfast, which he ate without appetite, he called Spring Creek Resort and the clerk put him through to Carter's room. In a voice still hoarse with sleep, Carter answered and the two set up an appointment for another meeting in mid-morning.

Carter hadn't asked whether Steadman had made his decision. The fact of his call, Steadman thought, was enough of a clue as to where he was heading.

"I didn't think I'd pass muster," Carter said, arriving on Steadman's porch a couple of hours after his call.

"Why would you think that?" Steadman asked.

"Investment banker from New York who had made a pile of dough." Carter said. "It sends off a message of acquisitive greed."

"Yes it does," Steadman agreed.

"Well, here we are again. Eyeball to eyeball. What's it going to be?"

"Do I have your word on what we discussed?" Steadman asked.

"You have that, Mr. Steadman. Upon my honor. You can take it to the bank."

"No subdividing. The land stays intact. The name stays."

"Agreed. On all three."

Carter held out his hand and Steadman took it. Both grips were strong as if the strength somehow was the measure of the promise. Steadman was relieved. The ritual of the handshake made him feel secure. He sensed he had struck a good and honest bargain in both Amy's name and his own.

"No second thoughts, Mr. Steadman?"

"None. Except that it will take me a month or two to clear out."

"No need to rush." Carter said, pausing for a moment, then chuckling. "We haven't discussed price."

"Just make it fair," Steadman said, certain that Carter had researched the comparables and knew the land's true value. He was far less interested in the money than in the fulfillment of Amy's wish.

"Will $3 million hack it?" Carter asked.

Steadman was stunned. The best offer he had gotten was $1.5 million. What in the world was he going to do with all that money? He considered it a cruel irony that all those years of hard-scrabble suffering to make ends meet should end in an embarrassment of riches for which he had no need.

If Amy was alive, he wondered, what would she have said? She was the one who ran the books for the ranch, and the very most they had ever had in the bank was $50,000 and that was only for a month or two after a cattle sale. It was far too late for money. He supposed that he would wind up giving most of it away to charity.

"That'll do fine," Steadman replied, feeling the constriction in his throat.

Carter nodded, and they shook hands again.

"And remember your promise," Steadman said.

"Done," Carter said.

Lawyers wrapped up the financial details, and Steadman arranged for an auction of various possessions that he would not need, keeping only those items that had sentimental value or were essential to the new life he planned for himself. He could not bear to attend the auction. Carter had told him to sell whatever he wanted.

The day he left the ranch for good was a day for tears. He felt hollow and deeply unhappy. With him went all the memories of the old life—Amy, his parents, the cows, the branding, the ranch hands and cowboys, his pets, all his history, days upon days of a good life lived. He could barely see the road through his tears.

By the time he had arranged to leave, it was November and he headed for the desert and bought himself a condominium in Phoenix, where he spent the winter. He hated it, made few friends and missed his beloved valley. In the spring, he went to Australia and New Zealand, then toured China. It was only mildly interesting to him.

Then he booked a world cruise on the QE II, which he hated, feeling out of place and unable to connect with people. He did not like the confinement of the boat, and even though he had booked a large stateroom, by his standards it was small and he felt claustrophobic. The fact was that he missed Jackson Hole.

Above all, he concluded that he was not a social person and had no skill in small talk. He essentially was a rancher and a cowboy, used to long silences and wide open spaces under the big sky. He felt as if he was marking time waiting for the grim reaper to reach his patch.

After two years of what he considered aimless wandering, he came back to the valley. Up to then, it would have been too painful to visit the Circle Bar S and see how Carter was faring. Memories were too fresh. But time somehow had reduced the prospect of pain, and his first act on flying into the Jackson airport was to rent a car.

Low clouds hung over the valley, and he couldn't see the old ranch from the air. The only familiar sight was the peak of the Grand, pushing out of the mist below as the plane punched though the clouds.

He planned to visit the ranch, ride around, see some of the old-timers and contemplate the idea of coming back to the valley, renting a place in town and spending his days in his old haunts telling stories of the past to those who were still alive.

The Circle Bar S, being north of town, was only a ten-minute drive from the airport, and with great anticipation and excitement, he drove south, then turned in toward the river, heading up beside the western edge of the airport.

He could not believe what met his gaze. Stone structures with metal lettering proclaiming "Circle Bar S Estates" were on both sides of the old ranch entrance that had been landscaped with spruce and aspen trees. The old road had been widened and paved with asphalt, and new roads crisscrossed the old pastures. A few bulldozers and backhoes were at work cutting into what had become full-blown sage meadows.

He felt a hollowness begin in the pit of his stomach and a cold sweat break out on his back, chilling him. How could this be? he asked himself. Stunned and confused, he drove the rented car to a spot near a man working a backhoe.

He got out of the car. His knees shook and his legs felt like jelly.

"What's happening here?" he asked the man operating the backhoe.

"Digging a foundation," the man said.

"Carter's house?" he managed to ask, foolishly clinging to that possibility.

"Hell no. Carter lives by the river," the man said, pointing to the stand of lodgepoles in the general direction of where his and Amy's house had stood.

"This a house for one of his kids?" Steadman asked.

"Where you been? He's got eighty going up. Lots sold out like hot cakes. Some are even turning over. Carter's made himself one big pile."

Steadman felt a thump in his chest and his breath came hard and shallow. He turned away from the man on the machine and, with effort, headed toward his car. He couldn't believe it. The man had promised and Steadman had believed in the promise.

He sat in the car for a long time. Somehow the knowledge had sapped his strength, and he needed to rest. He closed his eyes and felt tears stream down his cheeks.

"I'm so sorry, Amy. I'm so sorry," he repeated to himself over and over again.

After awhile, he felt strong enough to drive and he followed the old road to where his house once stood. He felt an incipient rage stirring inside him. He had been so confident that he knew men and their motives. How could he have made such a mistake?

Riding along the path of the old road, he passed through the familiar forest of lodgepoles, then into a long circling driveway to a log house of immense proportions. His old house was gone. Around the new house was lawn and, close by, a putting green complete with sand trap. In the distance, he could see another golf-hole flag fluttering in the breeze.

With what inner strength he could muster, he tamped down his rage, although he could not control his shaking legs as he walked up to the front door of the house and rang the buzzer. He knew that there was no way to reverse the process, but, for his own self-respect, he decided, he needed to confront Carter.

A young woman answered the door.

"Can I help you?"

"I would like to see Mr. Carter," Steadman said.

"He's in his study. He doesn't like to be disturbed. Is there anything I can do? I'm the housekeeper. Mrs. Carter is off on a shopping trip to New York."

"I'm afraid my business is with Mr. Carter," Steadman said, hearing the reediness in his voice.

"I really don't think. . . ."

"He'll see me."

The woman eyed him up and down with what he imagined was contempt. What business did this old fart have with Mr. Carter, she was probably thinking. She had closed the front door and he stood awkwardly waiting for it to open again.

When it did, Carter, dressed in plaid cowboy shirt, tight jeans, a belt with a large silver buckle, snakeskin cowboy boots and a fringed vest, stood in the doorway. He was smiling, and his hand was outstretched. Despite his rage, Steadman had no time to think and took the man's hand, remembering the last time he had taken it. Now it felt cold and clammy to his touch.

"Mr. Steadman. So good to see you. Come on in."

Steadman was not prepared for the hospitable welcome. He followed Carter into the house, a massive log structure filled with Western antiques, Western paintings mostly of cowboys pushing cattle, braving storms, slogging through mud, sitting around campfires. Others were images of painted Indian faces.

There were many pieces of log furniture and, on the walls, hung Indian artifacts. Sculptures large and small of wildlife and cowboys on horses adorned various spaces throughout the areas that he passed.

Steadman followed Carter into his large study, dominated by a massive carved desk and heavy leather chairs. Behind the desk was a huge painted landscape of a mountain setting.

"Drink?"

"No, thanks," Steadman said.

"Take a chair, Mr. Steadman. Make yourself at home."

Home? Steadman thought. He was appalled by the idea. Carter went behind his desk, lifted his fancy cowboy boots on its surface and clasped his hands behind his head.

"So what do you think?" Carter asked, still smiling, after a long silence.

"About what?" Steadman asked.

"The house, Mr. Steadman. Built in record time. Catch all that Western art work? Would you like a tour?"

"No, thanks, Carter."

"You back for a visit? Heard you had a place in the desert."

"I think you owe me an explanation."

"I do? For what?"

"You promised. We shook hands on it."

Carter scratched his chin and looked at Steadman.

"Conditions changed, Steadman. Opportunities arose. The county was changing the rules. I had no choice but to act before the door closed on the possibility. Just business, Steadman. Hell, you came out smelling like a rose."

"But you promised. We shook on it. I made it clear. I never would have sold you the place—you said you would never subdivide. . . ."

"I told you. An opportunity came up. I've got eighty lots in my master plan. People are gobbling them up. Really, Steadman, what kind of a dumb businessman would I be if I didn't seize the opportunity?"

"You said you hit your number," Steadman said. "You'd made enough money."

"Hell, can't be too thin or too rich," Carter chuckled.

Steadman felt the bile rise in his chest. His tongue felt dry and his anger made it impossible for him to respond. Instead, he just sat there, staring at Carter, his fancy boots on the carved desk.

"It was a condition of the sale," Steadman said finally, but his voice had weakened and he felt faint.

"You OK, Steadman?" Carter asked. "You look pale."

"And you, Carter? Are you OK? Don't you feel anything?"

"Me? What should I feel? We did business. And business is business. The trick in business is to recognize opportunity. I saw it from the beginning. I gave you double what the other bastards offered. You came out pretty good. Three mil on the barrelhead. Not bad for an old duffer with a few years left. You could have a ball. No heirs. You could spend it all. You should have no gripes, Steadman."

"You cheated me, Carter." Steadman said, his voice still reedy. He felt weak, defeated, defeated by age, defeated by greed.

Carter scowled, lifted his feet off the desk and stood up.

"I think this little meeting is over, Steadman. Your problem is you let emotion and sentimentality get in the way of your business sense. Hell, Steadman, this place is hot. It's discovered. The big money is rolling in. Money talks and bullshit walks. There's a feeding frenzy for land going on in this valley. Fortunes will be made. You old-timers were here all along. How come you didn't see it?"

With effort, Steadman stood up. Carter was probably right. Greed was too powerful to be opposed. The bad guys had won. The valley that he and Amy had lived in was over. Aubrey Steadman was over. He followed Carter out to the door, which Carter opened. Steadman started to walk outside. He was tired and wasn't sure he would make it to the car. Then he turned and faced Steadman, standing there in his fancy Western duds.

"You'll never be a true Westerner, Carter. All the cowboy clothes and pictures and Indian stuff and wildlife paintings and your big fancy log cabin won't make you a Westerner. Not a real one. You don't have what it takes inside."

Carter slammed the door, and Steadman walked unsteadily to his car. He wondered where he had found the strength to say the things he had just said.

Sitting behind the wheel waiting for his equilibrium to return, he looked up toward the mountain peaks of the Tetons.

"You're still beautiful," he thought. "I'm ashamed of what you have to put up with, watching us poor dumb mortals down here."

He turned on the ignition and headed back down the old ranch road, knowing he would never return.

# 2
# THE COWBOY EXPERIENCE

The ranch house had been built in the flats between the two buttes. Years ago, the original owners, descendants of homesteaders, had planted golden willow cuttings in a circle around the house; they had grown to a uniform height of about twenty-five feet, bushing out and filling in so that, from ground level, it was almost impossible to see beyond the perimeter to the pastures where the cattle grazed.

The upstairs bedrooms offered a view of the corral and outbuildings, which served as sleeping quarters for the hands, as well as the barns and repair shops for various ranch operations, most of which still were mysteries to Holbrook. He had promised himself to learn as much as he could about the workings of the ranch. So far, he hadn't, though he had maintained a pose of intense interest, asking pointed and, he hoped, intelligent questions of Bellows.

Bellows was the ranch manager, who had, thankfully, come with the purchase.

In his mind, Holbrook already had discounted the expected losses. He had bought the ranch less as a profit-making venture than as a fulfillment of Jan's Western fantasy. Not that he liked to lose money. As an investment banker, it was against all of his principles. Making money was his way of life.

But a few years ago, he had taken on a new wife—less than half his age—which gave him a broader view of living and allowed him to consider his financial interest in the ranch more a psychic investment in his and Jan's happiness. He approved of psychic investments, as long as the downside wasn't significant.

Jan's father had been a wrangler in Cheyenne, and although she admitted he had deserted the family early and was a drunk and a womanizer, she still had a romantic view of cowboys. She was four years old when her mother left Wyoming for New Jersey, and she had seen her father only a few times in her life. He had died of cirrhosis of the liver before he was thirty-five, but she continued to have a sentimental view of him as a misunderstood man, blaming her mother for what had become of him.

"He looked like Gary Cooper, that actor you see in old movies on the movie channel," she told him.

"Oh, that one," he had answered, as if he wasn't of age to remember seeing the actor in the movie theaters. You didn't have to have a Ph.D. in psychology to see where the fantasy had come from.

She was taking horseback lessons from Cleet, one of the cowboys, and walked around in cowboy boots, jeans and fringes, and wore a tan cowboy hat, side brims turned up.

"Don't you just love his name, Martin? Cleet. Sounds so Western. His last name is Hawkins."

"As in Sadie."

"No, Martin, as in Cleet. He's right out of central casting. Long-legged, small-hipped. Lots of yups and maams and he rolls his own cigarettes with one hand."

"There's a skill for you."

"Says he also wants to be a cowboy poet and listens to them on his Walkman."

"Is he a good horse teacher?"

"Yup."

"Won't be long before you're pushing cows yourself."

"Yup."

She was always up before him, tiptoeing around so as not to wake him, hurrying into her outfit and scurrying down the stairs to the corral to get on with her lessons. Recently, he had gotten up and watched them in the corral from the window of the bedroom. Cleet was exactly as she described—tall, small-hipped and long-legged, with a face tanned and weathered beyond his years.

Seeing Jan and Cleet together for the first time filled Holbrook with a vague sense of discomfort. She had brought out two mugs of steaming coffee, and they drank them sitting hunched over on the corral rail. They seemed to have developed an easy manner between them, smiling and laughing in the clear bright morning sun. Perhaps it was the sense of his own exclusion that troubled him.

He watched them a long time, until they finished their coffee, and Cleet helped her down from the corral rail, gripping her under her arms in a way that somehow didn't square with the relationship one should have with employees. He admitted to a brief pang of jealousy, but the memory of her enthusiastic lovemaking just hours before took the sting out of the thought. Hell, he decided, they were about the same age. There had to be some commonality in that.

She was twenty-five years old, and he had met her when she was twenty-one and he was fifty-five. At the time, she was an analyst trainee at one of the money-management firms with which he dealt and he had, inexplicably and unexpectedly, fallen in love with her. He hoped the feeling was mutual. She told him so, but he had learned to put a higher premium on behavior than on words. Up to now, she had given him no reason to doubt her.

He had been married to his first wife for nearly thirty years, and she had died suddenly in an automobile crash. Upon her death, he had the sense that he would never find another life's companion. All in all, his first marriage was a good one; it had produced two daughters who now were raising families of their own. They both thought he had lost his mind when he announced that he was marrying a woman less than half his age.

He paid no attention to their entreaties and dire warnings, figuring that they probably were thinking more of their inheritance than of his happiness. He knew this was a cynical attitude but he was disappointed in them and in the men they had married. Besides, what did they know of loneliness and a man's needs and the brief window that was life?

Jan made him forget his age. In fact, she made him feel younger in every way. He was stirred by her young body and her caring nature. She also made him laugh. He hadn't laughed much with his first wife. She was much more inhibited and restrained. He supposed that was what was meant by the generation gap.

"Age is only a state of mind," Jan assured him, although he knew better.

Holbrook did not consider himself a stupid man. In his business, evaluating the potential downside was more important than understanding the upside. He calculated he might have, if he stayed healthy, fifteen or twenty quality years with Jan. He had made it quite clear that he did not wish to have any more children, and she had been eager to agree.

"One baby is enough to take care of," she had told him with a smile and wink.

Naturally, he had her sign a prenuptial agreement, but it did exempt what wealth and possessions they might accumulate during their marriage.

This meant that upon his death she would be entitled to that portion of his estate that had been acquired during the time they were together. His daughters were well-provided for with what he had accumulated prior to his marriage to Jan.

Of course, he had had his lawyer put a number of protective caveats in the prenup document. He was a very cautious man with a healthy level of distrust. Jan had signed the agreement without raising any questions.

"I love you, Martin. That's the bottom line for me."

"For me, too, Jan. It's just a formality executed on my lawyer's advice. In our situation, it's important to have the financial ground rules carefully spelled out. Just in case. For your protection as well."

"When it comes to business and money, Martin, I'll defer to your judgment," she told him.

He also had calculated that he could partially compensate for the inevitable aging process by focusing on those of her perceived needs and desires that could be addressed through his wealth, like the ranch he had bought in Bondurant, Wyoming. He had set up an office in the ranch house and, with modern communications and computers, he figured he could spend at least six months at the ranch without going back East.

Jan was neither a spendthrift nor an acquirer of possessions. She spent very little. It was he who had bought her presents—including jewelry, clothes, and a Mercedes Sport Coupe—and had given her carte blanche to decorate their apartment on Park Avenue in Manhattan. The same would hold true when she started to fix up the ranch.

Actually, she protested his extravagance, but he assumed she was being coy and secretly was pleased with his many valuable gifts.

"You really shouldn't have, Martin," she told him. "Material things aren't my bag."

"I do it because I want to do it," he would reply. "It makes me happy to give you things. It is an expression of my love for you."

"It's not necessary, Martin. Love means giving of yourself, not giving things."

Nevertheless, she accepted his gifts and seemed to enjoy them.

She was tall and blonde and very well-made, with high breasts, wonderful legs and a supple body that looked great both dressed and undressed. Just observing her made him feel good. He was very proud to have her on his arm in public, although older women probably snickered behind his back. A man his age with a young girl like that! Sometimes she was mistaken for his daughter, but he didn't care.

As for the men his age, they probably were green with envy behind their snickers. Every time that Jan made those little gurgling sounds of pleasure during their lovemaking, he felt that he was soaring like a rocket above the Earth. That was more than enough compensation for any imagined ridicule.

He had made his fortune in the eighties. Like Jan, he was from humble beginnings. His dad had been a shoe salesman in a store in a small town in West Virginia, where he had been born. His father worked on commission and hated his job, and Martin had vowed never to work for other people—which he hadn't—but he still retained some of the vestiges of the economic denial and insecurity of his youth. He also thought it gave him a special insight into the motives of others and, for this reason, he was not a trusting man.

He couldn't keep himself from observing his wife and the young cowboy from his bedroom window. They appeared to be growing more familiar each passing day, and from their smiles and the way their body language expressed itself, he felt a growing sense of discomfort.

"Who is this Cleet fellow?" he asked the ranch manager one day, hoping that his inquiry sounded casual and off-the-cuff.

"Just a hand," Bellows replied. He had a deeply lined face and a drooping mustache that was beginning to go to gray, and he wore an old weathered and stained cowboy hat low over his forehead. Although Bellows usually looked directly into his eyes when he spoke, Holbrook noted that he turned his eyes away when he answered that question. Holbrook believed that if a man couldn't look you in the eye, he was hiding something.

"Where'd he come from?" Holbrook asked, shrugging as if what was said meant little.

"Fella just appeared. That's what they do. Just show up with a saddle and one change of clothes lookin' for work. Good worker, though. Knows his horses."

"Doesn't come with references?"

"You kiddin'?"

"Just a drifter then?"

"That's it. They just drift. They live by the code that being free is everything. Most work for a little while, then move on. Fact is, they're honest as the day is long. Some eventually settle down, guide folks on pack trips. Some just drift away like tumbleweed. Never see 'em again."

"Seems to be doing a good job teaching Mrs. Holbrook the mysteries of the horse," Holbrook said, watching the man's face. It didn't tell him much.

"Oh, they know their horseflesh," Bellows said, spitting into the scrub. The mention of the word flesh did not sit well with Holbrook, as if it was said deliberately to plant fear. Holbrook held in any sign that he was annoyed, figuring that Bellows resented him on principle. Probably considered Holbrook this rich dude from New York who didn't know a horse from a horse's ass.

He had been observing Jan and Cleet for a couple of weeks now, watching their routine of drinking coffee and sitting hunched on the corral rail, then saddling up and riding off toward the backcountry. Uncomfortable images were beginning to crowd into his mind as he tried to picture what they might be doing out there. He ridiculed these images as mere musings of an older man envious of the young, but try as he would, he couldn't eliminate them from his mind.

Usually, they were gone all morning, then Jan would come back into the house, bringing in the smell of horse and sweat and a big smile of joyful exhilaration.

"It was wonderful, Martin, riding in the backcountry under that big sky. We follow old game trails and Cleet points out the wonders of the natural world. We saw a herd of antelope today and watched a great blue heron along a stream bank spearing cutthroat trout. Gives you a new perspective on the life-and-death struggle of the natural world."

"When you get it figured out, let me know." Martin told

her with an edge of sarcasm that she had ignored or had sailed over her head.

"There's so much. . ." She paused, searching for the word. " . . .bigness out there. You can't imagine the sense of freedom you get riding in all that space."

Then she would shower and the cook would make them lunch and she'd go off to Jackson to shop, sometimes with him and lately without him.

In the afternoons, when Jan was gone, Holbrook would drive his four-wheel Jeep over the range ostensibly to look over the grazing cattle. What he really was looking for was Cleet. He never found him, which meant little since the ranch was a large spread and, without his asking Bellows, he would not have a clue as to Cleet's whereabouts. He chose not to ask.

He had moments when ugly suspicious thoughts would occupy his mind, and he was tempted to follow Jan into town. But he never gave in to that temptation, fearing that he would make some terrible discovery.

"You seem to be getting the hang of riding," Holbrook said to Jan one evening as they sat on the porch sipping white wine and watching the sun sink over the mountain range.

"It's fun, Martin," she had replied. "You should take it up. Cleet's a great teacher and he tells me I'll be ready soon to push cattle."

"That'll be something." Holbrook said, letting some time pass. "Bellows says this Cleet fellow is just a drifter." He waited for her reaction, watching her face with peripheral vision, searching for some change of expression that might give him a hint of what she was thinking.

He could detect nothing out of the ordinary, which only enhanced his suspicion. It wasn't exactly jealousy he was feeling, he noted to himself. More like sadness.

"All I know is that he's a pleasant person and a good riding teacher," Jan said.

"They just show up one day with a saddle asking for work," Holbrook said, still watching her. "They just drift around from one ranch to another."

"Cowboys are free spirits," Jan said.

"Sort of an anachronism," Holbrook said. "That world is over."

"Too bad," Jan sighed, looking into the distance, her eyes glistening in the last gasp of light. He wondered what she was seeing out there.

She was silent for a long time as if she were ruminating on that one thought. Then she spoke.

"Got a surprise, Martin," she said, brightening suddenly.

"A surprise?" He suddenly was gripped by panic.

"I've arranged a pack trip for us on the Wind River Range," she said. There was something tentative in the way she said it, as if she were waiting for the moment and had determined that this was it.

"Us?"

"Of course, us," she said laughing, slapping his thigh. "You and me."

"Up there alone?"

"Don't be silly, Martin. We can't do it alone. Cleet will be our guide. He knows the Winds and will make all the arrangements.

"Me, on a horse?" Holbrook said.

"We'll be riding trail horses so you won't have to have any special skills. Anybody can do it. It'll only be for three days, but I understand it's one of the great outdoor experiences."

She broke into a monologue about the Wind River, explaining that it extended for more than 100 miles, held forty summits higher than 13,000 feet, had the ten largest glaciers in the lower forty-eight and contained 1,600 lakes.

"It's like getting inside a post card," she concluded.

"What a wonderful surprise," he said, with a touch of sarcasm, shaking his head. He'd never been on a pack trip before and was genuinely put out by not having been asked before arrangements had been made. But he hid his agitation. He knew he wouldn't refuse, especially because it gave rise to the prospect that Jan might choose to go without him. She and Cleet alone. He couldn't bear that idea.

"You'll love it, darling. I hope you're not angry with me." She came over and kissed him on the lips and, for a moment, he felt secure again. Perhaps the images he was manufacturing in his mind were just so much hubris.

"Of course, we'll have to ask Bellows if he can spare Cleet for those days," Holbrook said as a kind of hedge. Secretly, he hoped Bellows would raise an objection.

"Oh, I've already gotten Bellows' permission. Cleet was due for a three-day holiday anyway."

"Bellows wasn't mad, was he?"

"Not at all. He thought it was a great idea."

Holbrook wondered why he would think that. He was beginning to imagine that others around the ranch also were suspecting that something was going on.

"You think I can do it?" Holbrook asked.

"Cleet has arranged for very fine horses who have done it hundreds of times. It'll be a gas. We'll be pitching tents and eating outdoors. Cleet says we'll be perfectly safe. He's done it many times. You'll love it, Martin. I guarantee it."

"That's good enough for me," Martin said. It wasn't really, but what choice did he have? He couldn't suggest that she go alone with Cleet, and he wouldn't want to dampen her excitement. Besides, he was letting his imagination run away with him.

"Think Cleet can handle a pack trip in the Wind River?" Holbrook asked Bellows a couple of days before they were set to leave.

"I'd say so," Bellows said, not looking him in the eye.

"Cleet apparently has been there many times before."

"So he says. And if they say something, it's probably the truth. These birds never lie. Also part of the code."

"And you think we're in good hands?"

"I'd say so."

"Never been on a pack trip." Holbrook said.

"It's rough country. But lots do it."

"Even an old fart like me."

Bellows didn't laugh, not even a little chuckle.

"Part of the cowboy experience," Bellows muttered.

They were standing in one of the work sheds where equipment repairs were made. Bellows went to a cabinet and took out a pistol in a leather holster.

"Might want to take this," he said. "It's a .45 Luger." He took it out of the holster, checked it, took out a clip filled with cartridges and showed it to Holbrook. "Clip goes in like this." He demonstrated, sliding in the clip, taking it out again. Then he showed him how to work the safety and how to aim and shoot. Holbrook tried it, sited, then Bellows corrected his position.

"Do I really need this?" Holbrook asked.

"Actually, it's government land and it's supposed to be illegal to carry a weapon in. I'd say better safe than sorry, though. You never know what you get up there. Better safe than sorry."

Holbrook packed the pistol in a new duffel bag that Jan had purchased for the trip, but said nothing to her about what Bellows had given him. Carrying the weapon on the pack trip seemed a perfectly logical idea. But it did plant a thought in his head that he wished had not been put there.

The night before the pack trip, Jan and Holbrook made love. For him, it was a kind of test, and he detected nothing amiss. Her lovemaking was as enthusiastic as ever and he assured himself that he had no business thinking what he was thinking. After all, he was a man who normally judged people by their behavior, not by what his imagination had concocted.

They drove out to Pinedale, then headed east to the Green River Lakes trailhead, towing horse trailers in two pickups they had borrowed from the ranch. Cleet had brought three trail horses and two mules to haul the tents and food supplies. Expertly, Cleet loaded and secured the mules, then buckled the saddle on the horse he had chosen for Holbrook—a black horse that had seen better days. The horse had a glazed look in its eyes and seemed bored and indifferent.

"Guess the black means I'm one of the bad guys," Holbrook joked. Cleet chuckled pleasantly and proceeded to help him into the stirrups, then push him upward into the saddle.

"Now just hold onto the reins like this," Cleet said, demonstrating how to turn and stop the horse and how to get him to back up and go forward. "Just dig your heels into his belly when you want him to go. He'll do the rest."

Holbrook, who was overweight, knew he looked clumsy and awkward getting on the horse. He watched as Jan and Cleet lifted themselves smoothly onto their saddles.

Cleet, holding the lead rope to the mule, led the riders across the Green River Lakes bridge, through meadows, fording streams, then into the mountain trails. Holbrook followed the mules and Jan held up the rear. They moved slowly, heading in an ever-ascending spiral up the switchback trails, Cleet looking back occasionally to check on their progress. Holbrook felt a growing resentment at the sense of command and authority Cleet was exhibiting.

Up on his horse, leading the mules, Cleet appeared young, fearless and heroic while Holbrook felt cowardly, clumsy and old, knowing he was sitting on his horse awkwardly and feeling aches in his knees and back. He dared not look behind him, though he heard Jan's horse's hoofs clattering on the rocks. He had no illusions about how he fared by comparison to Cleet.

As they moved higher into the mountains, the trail grew narrower and the switchbacks more angular. A quick glance below showed a sheer drop into the canyons, and Holbrook could not help but speculate how dependent they were on the sure-footedness of the horses as they clattered up the switchbacks. One bad step and horse and rider would be history.

Jan grew animated as they moved higher, pointing out rock formations, waterfalls, circling birds and wildflowers. Obviously, she had acquired a great deal of knowledge about these natural phenomena on her backcountry treks with Cleet. Holbrook expressed appropriate wonder at the various things she referred to, but was too scared, pained and anxious to be truly appreciative.

They rode for four hours before Cleet led them off the trail into a shady grove near a gurgling stream. Holbrook managed to get off his horse, but upon hitting the ground, his knees buckled and he fell into the tall grass. Cleet came to his rescue and helped him up, adding to his humiliation.

"Take some aspirin, Mr. Holbrook," Cleet suggested, signaling to Jan, who reached into her pocket and brought out a bottle of aspirin. She shook out three tablets and handed them to Holbrook, who washed them down with water from his bottle. The idea of having to take the aspirin diminished him even more.

Then the three of them sat on a fallen log and ate ham sandwiches that Cleet produced, washing them down with water. The sun was bright and hot, but occasional cloud puffs masked the sun and cooled things off momentarily. Holbrook looked at his black horse, neck stretched into the grass as it munched, and wondered how much longer it would be before they reached a campsite. He felt too cowardly to ask.

They mounted and continued their journey upward, traversing still more switchbacks. The aspirin had eased the pain in Holbrook's knees and back, leaving him to fester instead with his psychic pain and a growing sense of inadequacy. He tried to shake it, using his own standard of comparison.

In his world, he assured himself, he was powerful, rich, successful. He could manipulate people and make them do his bidding. If he chose—which he rarely did—he could make them cringe with fear. He could buy and sell this Cleet a thousand times over.

He already had shown himself to be weak and old in the face of their youth and strength. The comparison gnawed at him. He felt redundant and unwelcome, especially when he watched the two golden-haired, slim-hipped people talking in what seemed like low whispers, laughing occasionally, exhibiting an easy camaraderie.

As the day wore on and he grew more and more tired, his mind began to seize on wildly ominous forebodings. He was vulnerable up here alone with these two young people. It wouldn't take much to push his horse into a canyon and send him hurtling to certain death. Hell, he thought, there were any number of ways in which he could be dispatched, and it would be hard to prove, considering the natural dangers inherent in this place, that his demise would have been deliberate.

Occasionally, he would force himself to turn and look at Jan's face. Seeing her, offering a broad smile and a wink, gave him only temporary reassurance. But his mind would not give him any respite from his dire imaginings. With him out of the way, she would have enough money for Cleet and her to live a pretty good life. He rebuked himself for such a thought. He had no proof of this.

By the time they reached the campsite that Cleet had chosen, Holbrook's mind was reeling with all sorts of terrible possibilities. The pain had come back, but he managed to dismount without falling.

"Why not rest, Martin?" Jan said, "Cleet and I will pitch the tents and set up the camp."

He resented both the words and the thought, but her advice was well-taken. He was exhausted. Nodding, he sat on a log and watched as Jan and Cleet pitched the tents, then Cleet turned out the horses in a nearby pasture and hobbled them. When he came back, he set up the cooking grate and began to prepare the dinner. Jan brought out a couple of bottles of white wine and went off toward the stream, apparently to cool them.

Watching them doing what seemed like preassigned tasks, he felt a pang of resentment. He had been given no tasks to do.

"Is Cleet your real name?" Holbrook asked as he observed the young man lay out the steaks and put a pot of water over the grate fire.

"Clayton," the young man said. "From Clayt, it went to Cleet."

"Where did you grow up?"

"Kansas."

"You're a long way from Kansas."

"Yup."

"Always wanted to be a cowboy, did you?"

"Yup."

"No money in it, though. Not exactly what you would call a lucrative profession."

"Nope."

"For a guy who wants to be a cowboy poet, you sure are a man of a few words."

Cleet smiled and shrugged.

"I don't much like jawin' about myself. But I do like them cowboy poets tellin' it like it is. I don't care a rat's ass about money." He had been hunched over the grate fire and he stood up suddenly and spread his arms. "Hell, I got this. What more is there?"

The words were spare but Holbrook did get the message. There were people who did prefer the outdoor life, and he knew there were people who didn't give a rat's ass about money. He didn't begrudge him that.

They drank the cold, tart white wine before dinner, then opened a couple of reds and ate the steaks and vegetables that Cleet had prepared. Jan talked about what they had planned for tomorrow—fishing a stream that Cleet had pointed out on the map. Jan had brought along the fly-fishing rod Holbrook had bought her; she was going to fish for cut-throat and hoped to catch one legal enough for them to eat.

"Expect some ranger will suddenly pop up and cite you?" Holbrook asked. He had drank more wine than he was used to and felt an edge of nastiness begin inside him.

"It's not that, Martin. It's the idea of preserving the stock. You're not supposed to take young trout."

"How do you feel about that, Cleet?"

"People take the young ones, next thing you know there won't be no trout."

"A couple of do-gooders we got here," Holbrook said. He felt slightly tipsy and it had put an angry bite into his mood. In the investment-banking business, ecologists were known to have gone too far in promoting regulations. Holbrook wasn't a fanatic about that either way, but his mood had turned sour.

"Blind greed could destroy all this," Jan said, waving her arms as Cleet had done earlier.

"We were talking about one lousy illegal trout and you guys are making this a federal case. People need natural resources to live the good life and will have to get them one way or another."

He felt his nastiness rising and took their mention of greed as a personal insult, as if he was somehow being character- ized as a despoiler of the land, a robber baron, a person interested only in accumulating wealth at everyone else's expense.

"You people are full of shit," he said, his tongue feeling heavy for the drink.

"Martin!" Jan cried. Cleet shrugged, got up and started to gather the plates.

"I'm turning in," Martin said, realizing the state he was in.

"I'll help Cleet clean up," Jan said.

"You do that," Holbrook barked. He staggered off into the woods to urinate, then crawled into his tent. Jan had set up two single sleeping bags, side by side. Holbrook, still angry, crawled into one of them and closed his eyes.

Lying there in his clothes, his irritation still raw, he felt a growing sense of harassment. It was then that he remembered the pistol in his duffel bag. Reaching over, he felt for it in the dark, unzipped it and fished around for the Luger, then pulled it out and tucked it into his sleeping bag. Feeling it there beside him somehow eased his fears, and he fell asleep.

Suddenly, he opened his eyes. His first sensation was the bulk against his thigh. Reaching down, he felt the leather of the holster and quickly recovered his sense of time and place. He eased himself partially out of the sleeping bag and looked over to where Jan's sleeping bag had been unrolled. Reaching out, he patted it and noted that it was empty.

His head was pounding and he looked at his wristwatch. As near as he could figure, he had been asleep for two hours. What had awakened him? Where was Jan? Reaching for the holster, he removed the pistol and eased himself out of the sleeping bag.

Soon he found himself listening to the sounds of the night, noting that the loudest sound he heard was the beating of his own heart. A sense of fear and abandonment began to assail him and he knew that he was not living in his imagination now. With shaking fingers, he clicked off the pistol's safety.

He heard low voices coming closer, then Jan's voice and the lilting sound of her laughter. Peering into the darkness, he saw the outline of two figures walking toward the camp. Seeing them, he felt a rising bile of hot anger. Gripping the pistol, he leveled the sight in the direction of the sound.

Tears obscured the view and he felt a deep sob grow in his chest. His hand was too unsteady to hold the pistol and, although he wanted to pull the trigger, he had the presence of mind to realize the futility of the act. Lowering the gun, he silently slipped back into the sleeping bag.

He was shaking and his lips were chattering, as if a deep chill suddenly had taken possession of his body. He noted, too, that the coldness on his cheeks was simply the evaporation of his tears.

At that moment, he believed implicitly that he was being confronted with a potential disaster and he had no idea how to cope with it. It was the oldest story in the world. He was convinced that he had been betrayed by his wife. He was now that ever-comical figure, the cuckolded husband, made to appear ridiculous even to himself. But then, what had he expected? Chronology was inescapable. He saw it coming. Perhaps he had willed it as a kind of exercise to test her temptation.

What hurt even worse was the manner in which he believed she had concealed the betrayal, continuing to play the role of the loving, eager wife while spending a great deal of her time rolling in the hay with her cowboy lover. He felt a sense of total humiliation. And he was certain that everyone around the ranch knew what was going on.

He speculated that he was probably the talk of Bondurant and Jackson—the rich idiot with the wife who was screwing a cowboy. He believed he knew now what lay behind Bellows giving him the pistol. Bellows had seen the writing on the wall, the danger Holbrook was in. The pistol, Holbrook decided, was intended either to be an instrument of self-defense or rough justice. He wasn't sure which.

He heard her come into the tent and felt her inspecting his face to confirm that he was asleep. He kept his eyes closed and heard her remove her clothes and slip into her sleeping bag.

How was he expected to react to this? Marriage was a pledge of faithfulness. He had been faithful and that was exactly what he had expected from his wife, whatever her age, however much younger she was than him. Then he remembered that one of the caveats his lawyer had inserted into the prenuptial agreement was that, if she was ever found to be unfaithful, she would forfeit everything. The memory calmed him somewhat. It validated his distrust of human nature.

He fell into a kind of near-sleep, tossing and turning in the narrow confines of the sleeping bag. He awoke at sunrise feeling stiff and exhausted. He felt the pistol at his side, reached for it, then slipped the holster through his belt, where it would be clearly visible. Jan still slept tucked deeply into the sleeping bag, her head barely visible.

He had resolved nothing in his mind, except that, considering the circumstances, he had better be wary. He patted the holster. Hell, he was an easy target out here in the wilderness, a sitting duck.

If they had anything in mind, at least with the pistol visible, it might have a dampening effect on their plans. In an odd way, his possession of the pistol gave him a sense of renewed potency.

When he came out of the tent, Cleet was squatting near the grate making a pot of coffee. The water had just started to boil and he threw a couple of handfuls of coffee grounds on the boiling water and put on the top.

"Cowboy coffee," Cleet said when Holbrook came up to where he was squatting. Then Cleet laid strips of bacon on the frying pan, on top of which he put slices of white bread. Holbrook stood over him, watching the spectacle, hearing the coffee pot bubble. Soon the aroma of coffee hit the early morning air.

In a little while, the bacon began to pop and sizzle in the pan and the rich bacon smell joined with the coffee aroma.

"How do you like your eggs?" Cleet asked, looking up toward where Holbrook was standing. He hadn't shaved, and his beard was coming in blonde. Holbrook noted that the color of his eyes seemed to match the cerulean blue of the sky and his teeth shone white and dazzling as they caught morning sunbeams shafting through the trees.

Handsome son-of-a-bitch, Holbrook thought, knowing he himself looked gray and sallow in this light. But certainty had toughened him, and the weight of the pistol on his hip gave him confidence, as if somehow possession of the pistol evened the distance between age and youth. He was determined to show them he was not ready to turn over and surrender.

"Sunny-side up," Holbrook said.

If Cleet saw the pistol on his hip, he made no comment and went on with his cooking. He poured some of the bacon fat into another pan, then cracked two eggs and popped them onto the bacon grease.

"Smells great," Jan said, coming up behind them, just as Holbrook put a fork to his eggs, which Cleet had served to him with bacon and greasy toast on a metal plate. Beside him, on a flat rock, Cleet had placed a mug of the thick black "cowboy" coffee.

"Your buddy here is quite a cook," Holbrook said, raising the metal coffee mug toward Cleet in a kind of toast. "Hang the cholesterol. What's a clogged vein or two among friends?"

Even to Holbrook, his comment sounded strangely sarcastic, which had not been his original intent. But in the light of day, he was not inclined to wallow in his shame. He did not look at his wife's face to ascertain her reaction. At that moment, he was thinking about how he would get out of this situation alive.

"I'm glad you're feeling OK this morning, Martin," Jan said.

"Nothing worse than a mean drunk," Holbrook said.

"You were dead to the world when I got in," Jan said.

"Took me awhile to get to sleep," Holbrook said casually, watching Jan's face, seeing a sudden tic begin in her jaw that he hadn't seen before.

"We stayed up awhile to watch the stars," Jan said. Covering her bases, Holbrook thought. Liar, he thought. Lousy liar.

"Martin," Jan said suddenly. "What is that thing around your waist?"

"Oh that," he said. "Bellows gave it to me, just in case."

"Just in case of what?" Jan asked.

"In case I needed it."

"What for?"

Holbrook shrugged.

"You never can tell."

Cleet chuckled.

"Take that thing off, Martin," Jan said.

"Hell, makes me feel like one of those movie cowboys. Like Gary Cooper. He always had a pistol in a holster," Martin said.

"Don't be ridiculous," Jan said. She had turned ashen and looked genuinely disturbed. He noted that she had stolen a glance at Cleet and Cleet had raised his eyes to the sky.

"This little baby is going to remain right on my hip," he said, patting the holster, hoping it sent them a message.

After declining to go fly-fishing with them, Holbrook went into the tent and, dropping the flaps, watched them through the slit as they cast their lines into the stream, occasionally getting a strike. Jan squealed with excitement as they hauled in the catch and netted it, determining its size. They kept the legal ones and threw the others back into the stream.

He observed them, seeing them whispering together, then looking toward his tent, probably to see if he was watching them, but taking no bold chances. He supposed he needed to see them in action, a painful idea but necessary. He needed Jan to know that he knew for sure and, therefore, that she couldn't truthfully deny her action. Even though, in a legal sense, if it came to that, it would be his word against theirs. Nevertheless, he had learned in his business life that knowledge of the real truth had a power of its own.

Finally, he decided that they might be too cautious to try a daylight escapade, so he stretched out on the sleeping bag and, while thinking about what further course of action to pursue, he dozed off.

When he awoke, the sun was lower in the sky, and hearing movement outside the tent, he observed Jan and Cleet preparing dinner. Trout was sizzling in the frying pan and corn was boiling in a pot of water.

"I didn't have the heart to wake you, Martin," Jan said, her eyes noting the pistol in its holster on his hip. "Still wearing that silly thing?"

"Yup," Holbrook said, shooting a glance at Cleet.

"I hate those things," Jan said.

"Looks like you had a good fishing day," Holbrook said. "I hope they're all legal. Wouldn't want to think you stepped out of line here."

He was deliberately being more pointed in his hints. He had decided to let out a little line at a time, just enough to keep them wondering if he really knew what was going on.

What puzzled him most was why Jan would risk losing everything for this cowboy drifter. He had always assumed that she knew the rules of the game, knew what being unfaithful would mean. He was disappointed and saddened not only by her conduct, but in her judgment and her intelligence. She was being a fool, idiotic. As for her cowboy boyfriend, he was probably licking his chops and counting his money.

Holbrook knew exactly how he intended to deal with her once they returned to civilization. Like a bad investment, he would scuttle it, take his losses. He would turn her out, order her to leave his bed and board, with nothing more than the clothes on her back. Fini! His daughters had been right. He had been a stupid old fart.

Before and during the meal, Holbrook was cautious about the wine they were pouring, accepting refills, but spilling it out when they turned their eyes away. He was not going to let himself get tipsy and pass out as he had the night before.

He listened to her talk about their fly-fishing expedition and Cleet's praise for her skill. Obviously, he had taught her to fish during their forays into the backcountry. At what he considered the appropriate time, Holbrook excused himself and, imitating a slight stagger, made his way back to his tent. But this time he was dead sober.

He watched them through the slit in the tent flaps as they cleaned up, putting out the fire and plunging the area into darkness. He heard them whispering together, then watched as they moved out of sight, although he could still hear their voices but couldn't make out what they were saying. Then their voices faded, although occasionally he heard Jan's soft laughter.

After awhile, he couldn't hear a thing, but he continued to wait. Then, suddenly, it might have been an hour after he had begun his vigil, he heard low voices again. He stuck his head out of the tent and listened. Muffled human sounds were coming from Cleet's tent. So there it was, he thought. Proof positive.

Holding the pistol, he moved cautiously out of his tent and toward the sound of the faint voices in Cleet's tent. As he crossed the space between the tents, he felt his anger build. They were deliberately flaunting their affair, throwing it in his face, rubbing his nose in it.

He drew closer to the tent, listened, heard muffled voices. He felt an adrenaline rush as he moved toward the tent, pistol in hand. He stopped for a moment to make sure the safety was off. As he got close to the tent, he noted that the flaps were down. He paused for a moment, but the sounds from within were now obscured by the heavy pounding of his heart.

As he stood before the closed flaps of the tent, he felt a wave of blind anger engulf him, and he pushed aside the flaps, saw the bulked sleeping bag and the sudden movement inside, then leveled the gun and fired once.

He heard the grunt of pain and the scream almost at the same moment.

"Dumb sumbitch," Cleet cried, literally jumping out of the sleeping bag and crawling to the tent's entrance, lifting himself and hopping around grunting and cursing. Then he heard Jan's voice outside.

"Oh, no. Oh, no."

"Crazy bastard," Cleet cried. "Dumb sumbitch."

Holbrook had let the pistol drop to the ground beside the sleeping bag, where it hit some object emitting a human sound. He bent down and picked it up. It was a Walkman, still operating.

"Have you lost your mind, Martin?" Jan said from behind him. She picked up the Walkman and clicked off the sound.

"I thought . . ." Holbrook began, but his throat constricted.

"God almighty," Jan said. "Where is the pistol?"

But her eyes found it before he could get any words out and she picked it up, along with a flashlight that was lying beside the sleeping bag, then went out of the tent. Holbrook followed her outside. Cleet was propped against a tree trunk.

His pants' leg was rolled up, and he was inspecting a gash in his calf.

"No bone hit," Cleet said to Jan, crouching beside him. "Just a graze. First aid kit's in my duffel."

She moved quickly into the tent and brought out the first aid kit. Cleet opened it and took out antiseptic, bandages and tape, and Jan helped him dress the wound.

"I'm so damned sorry," Holbrook whined.

"Dumb shit," Cleet said. "What the hell did you think was going on in there?"

"I overreacted. Forgive me."

"You could have killed him," Jan said. "And me. Hell, I was coming back from nature's call. You might have thought I was a bear or something."

"I'm really sorry," Holbrook said. "Really sorry."

"You are one dumb sumbitch," Cleet said. He finished dressing the wound, rolled down his pants leg and stood up, He took the pistol from Jan, pulled out the clip and flung pistol and clip in different directions.

"I feel awful about this, Cleet," Jan said.

"Ain't your fault."

"We'll head out tomorrow. Get you to a doctor."

"Just send me the bill," Holbrook said. He felt a terrible emptiness inside of him. Cleet grunted and limped into his tent.

"How could you?" Jan said when they got back to their tent.

"What can I say?" Holbrook said, stretching out on his sleeping bag. He felt himself getting the shakes and his breathing was coming fast. He really felt his age now.

"You've ruined a wonderful experience, Martin."

"I sure did," Holbrook said. He felt just as Cleet had characterized him, like a dumb sumbitch. "I feel like hell, Jan," he said after awhile. She had crawled into the sleeping bag and turned her back toward him.

"You should," she muttered.

He lay there on top of the sleeping bag for a long time, wondering if it would ever be the same between him and Jan again. Nobody had mentioned a motive for his action. He'd leave it at that, offering no further explanation. After all, he had never raised the point, never hinted at the turmoil going on inside of him, never accused her of infidelity, never revealed the extent of his jealousy. Thank God, he hadn't killed the poor bastard. As he went over the potential consequences in his mind, he shuddered. This was one close shave with destiny. He hoped he could make it up with Jan.

He was still shaky when he awoke. Jan was already up, helping Cleet break camp. They had already struck the cooking things and packed away Cleet's tent. He looked pale and was limping around, obviously still in some pain.

"You OK, Cleet?" Holbrook asked when he came out of the tent.

"Yup," Cleet replied, striking Holbrook's tent, folding it and laying it in the canvas sheet. He and Jan rolled it up and secured it on the mule. When they had finished, Jan handed Holbrook a sandwich and a warm can of soda.

"You think he'll be OK?" Holbrook asked when Cleet was out of earshot.

"We redressed the wound. Doesn't look infected. He'll be fine, Martin."

"We'll have a doctor look at it," Holbrook said.

"No way. How will we explain a gunshot wound?"

He hadn't thought of that.

"It was an accident," Holbrook said.

"Was it, Martin?" Jan said.

They mounted the horses and headed downward, Cleet

leading the way as before, Jan next in the line and Holbrook
bringing up the rear. Getting down was tough going. No
one spoke. Holbrook loaded himself up on aspirin, then
tried ignoring his own pain. Considering what Cleet was
going through because of Holbrook's own stupid act, he
felt he deserved the punishment. Periodically, they rested,
ate sandwiches and watered the horses.

By late afternoon, they saw a sign saying they were six
miles from the trailhead. Thank the Lord, Holbrook sighed
to himself. Soon this nightmare would be over. The trail
widened as they neared the trailhead, and Jan slowed and
pulled up beside him. Cleet continued in the lead.

"I know why you shot him, Martin," Jan said.

"Can't we just forget about it, Jan?" Holbrook said.

"Never, Martin. I'll never forget about it."

"You don't understand."

"Yes I do, Martin. You distrusted me. You thought I was
unfaithful, that I had violated my marriage vows."

"It's best forgotten, Jan."

"You did think that, didn't you, Martin?"

"Let's leave it alone."

"You thought I was screwing him, having the ultimate
cowboy experience, didn't you?"

"Maybe others thought it, too." Holbrook said, sorry that
he had been goaded into saying that. Jan smiled and shook
her head.

"So you did think that?"

"I told you. Leave it alone."

"How can I live with someone who doesn't trust me?"

He felt his heart jump in his chest.

"Haven't I been damned good to you, Jan? I love you.
You know that. OK, I went nuts with jealousy. Considering
the circumstances . . . "

"What circumstances?"

"Never mind. It's too difficult to explain."

It wasn't really. Cleet was a young, handsome, heroic figure, a cowboy, stuff of legends and fantasies, and she was a young beautiful woman married to a much older man. It wasn't exactly unnatural to think what he thought.

From where they were riding, they could see the trailhead and the two pickups and the horse trailers. They rode on silently for awhile.

"I'm leaving you, Martin," she said.

It was not unexpected. There seemed no point in demeaning himself with argument.

"You'll get nothing," he said, unhappy with his malice, but thinking it necessary to, at the least, salvage his dignity and his old sense of authority.

"I know, Martin. It doesn't matter."

"Don't care a rat's ass about money, do you?"

"Not yours," she said. She wasn't one for sour notes, but this had hit her hard.

Again he felt a gnawing emptiness descend. He had no idea how to handle the situation, knowing in his heart it was impossible to woo her back. He felt his emotions on the razor's edge of fear and anger.

"All right," he said, seeing the trailhead looming a few yards ahead. "One question, though."

"Ask away," Jan replied. He could see that she had made peace with herself about her decision.

"Did you . . . with Cleet?"

She looked at him and smiled.

"There's my legacy for you, Martin, the great unanswered question," she said, kicking her horse and catching up with Cleet.

# 3
# *TAKING LEAVE*

 "Something is wrong," Alice said. "Something is terribly wrong."

She had sprung up in bed as if she had been frightened by a nightmare.

"We've been through that, Alice," Charles said.

Alice got out of bed and began to pace the floor of their small bedroom. It would be the last night they would be sleeping here. Tomorrow they would be leaving Jackson for Portland, Oregon. Charles had packed up the family's belongings in a large panel truck he had rented.

"I don't think I can do it, Charlie," Alice said.

"Don't talk so loud. The kids will hear."

"They're not stupid, Charlie. They don't want to leave, either. Leave their friends, their school. Leave this beautiful place where they grew up."

She felt the rage begin again inside of her. Why did this

have to happen? Why? Why? Why? As if he had read her mind, Charles, now sitting up on the bed, spoke.

"Economics, Alice. Pure economics. We've been through it over and over. We just can't make it here."

Alice taught third grade and worked the evening shift as a waitress at the Alpenhof Restaurant in Teton Village. Charles drove a truck for United Parcel Service by day and worked part time in the fly-fishing department at Jack Dennis. Charles had found a job in Portland as a supervisor for a trucking company at double the salary he calculated for his two jobs, and Alice had applied for a teaching job at a private school at a considerable raise. They told her she probably would be hired. Both were college graduates and had met at the University of Wyoming at Laramie.

"Maybe we want too much, Charlie," Alice said.

"Alice, we're exhausting ourselves. We're not making it. The valley has changed. It's not like when you grew up here and your family owned the ranch and got by. You can't look back anymore. Your day is over here."

"I don't know if I can hack it, Charlie."

"It's too late for regrets, Alice. The house is sold. The truck is packed. We're heading for Portland."

He got out of bed and embraced her.

"It's not the end of the world. Portland is a great city. There'll be opportunity for our kids. Hell, look at you, born and bred here and now we can't afford to live here. It's nothing more than a rich man's playground now. We'll get a fresh start."

"I don't want a fresh start, Charlie. This is my place."

Charles knew, of course, that there was a lot of truth to that statement. Alice did define herself by Jackson Hole. Her great grandparents had homesteaded here, had once owned nearly 1,000 acres. Her grandparents had ranched on the property and her parents after them. Unfortunately, during hard times, her grandparents, then her parents, had to sell off the land piece by piece. There was no more left.

"Change is difficult to accept, Alice," Charles said, brushing back her hair. "My place is here beside you. Wherever you and the kids are is my place." They had been married for fifteen years and had three children. Charles had been brought up in Casper, where his father still worked for one of the oil companies.

Alice's parents had died within two years of each other. She had been an only child. Perhaps it was her mother's death, after her father's, that helped set the move in motion. The land was gone as well.

"I don't want to go, Charlie," Alice said.

"We'll have a good life in Portland, Alice. I promise."

She insinuated herself out of his embrace and walked over to the window. Outside, she could see the canopy of stars and the outlines of the Teton mountain peaks. This was her daily view since childhood and she had never lost her enthusiasm for the grandeur and mystery of it.

"My soul is in this place."

"I know, darling. I know."

"How can I leave it?"

"You can, Alice. We've been through that."

They had, of course, been through it ad infinitum. They had gone over all the pros and cons.

"There's no future here for us or the kids, Alice," Charlie had explained. "Oh, there are service jobs. Lots of them. But what have the kids to look forward to? Sure, they'll go to college like us, but will they come back here? And if they did, to what? To being a waitress or a river guide or a ski instructor. Or, like me, a delivery man."

"It has its compensations," Alice said. "The air, the beauty of the mountains, the wilderness." She continued to look out of the window. "Starry skies and wildflowers and wildlife and wonderful white snow."

"That's a sentimental argument, Alice. Face the reality."

"Depends how you define the good life. We had nothing back when I grew up. But we had land and this glorious place."

"Your land is gone, Alice."

"They should never have sold the land. Never."

"If they could have, they would have kept it. Don't be hard on them."

"I loved them, Charlie, but they should never have sold the land."

During the last few years, it had become an obsession. The value of the land once owned by the family had soared. What once fetched double digits now ran into the hundreds of thousands, and the influx of new people was bidding the prices even higher.

"We could have been millionaires," Alice said. "Why couldn't they have seen that?"

"Who would have thought a high valley like this, so remote and cold in winter, would be in such demand?" Charlie said.

"Some locals held on. They're rich now. Look at us. We're going into exile."

"That's the wrong way to look at it. We're going in search of opportunity."

"We're being banished from our land," Alice said. "They were fools to sell so early. Fools." She paused and sighed. "God I loved them but they were such fools."

"There's no point in harping on that, Alice," Charles said. "You can't look back."

"Yes, I can," Alice protested. "Especially today."

"It's too late, Alice. We're all set to go."

"I don't want to go to a strange place. I don't want to go to Portland. I want to stay right here."

"Please, Alice. Lower your voice."

"I don't want to go to Portland."

"We're committed, Alice. We've sold the house."

"We can buy another one."

"We barely got enough out of this one to buy another house here. I showed you the arithmetic. When all was said and done, what did we clear? Twenty grand."

"You sold it too cheap."

"It was on the market for a year, Alice," Charlie reminded her. He knew what she was going through and he was determined to be gentle, although inside he was frightened and depressed, but he could not show her that.

The fact was that he hated to leave the valley as well. But he did not want her to think of him as a failure. He forced himself to be optimistic, and he was convinced that a better economic future beckoned in Portland for all of them.

In Jackson, they were getting economically marginalized, crowded out. With both of them working two jobs, they were growing tired. Tension in the family was increasing. Their kids needed them around, especially now when they were on the cusp of the uncertain teenage years. Logic and common sense, he believed, was on his side.

"Portland is a nice town, manageable. It's not New York or LA."

"It's not Jackson Hole," Alice said.

"Granted," he replied. "But it's a nice town."

Alice, still watching the stars, turned suddenly facing him.

"I can't leave," she said.

"Alice," he said, feeling a sense of frustration and rage

begin inside of him. "It's too late for us to undo. I have to report for work on Wednesday. I've quit both jobs. So have you. We've sold our house. We're packed and ready. You can't do this to me."

"The kids don't want to leave, either."

"Why are you doing this, Alice?"

"I'm not leaving."

"Now you're getting ridiculous. Really Alice. You're pushing the envelope here. It's over. Get it through your head. Someday maybe we'll come back. Maybe we'll hate Portland so much, we'll come back. Maybe when the kids are grown we'll come back. . . ."

He shook his head in despair and went back to bed, turning his face away from her. He was angry and depressed. Then he heard movement behind him. Turning, he saw that she was dressing.

"Where are you going?"

"Out."

"It's four in the morning."

"I know."

"Where are you going?"

"I'm not sure."

"Jesus, Alice. Don't do this to me."

He heard her move out of the room, then out the front door. Soon after, he heard the car's motor turn over. Moving swiftly, he ran out of the front door but by then the car had been driven out of sight.

They lived south of town, and she drove east through the darkened center of town. The town square, its ribbon of antlers and old cottonwoods and lodgepoles growing in its center, was exactly where it had always been. She also could recognize the Wort Hotel, the movie theater and the drug store. But everything else had changed.

Art galleries had proliferated, selling paintings to tourists, many of them glorifying cowboys and Indians. Not that it mattered. She couldn't afford any of them. Chain stores were lined up around and near the square: Polo, Gap, Pendleton, Benetton, Eddie Bauer. Elsewhere was a Kmart, Albertsons, and other chain stores, and, of course, the gaggle of fast-food operations.

Commercial individuality was fast disappearing. Jackson was becoming homogenized, its uniqueness compromised by the march of so-called progress. Was she deliberately looking to be critical? Did she need some excuse to ease her exit?

For a brief moment, she felt displaced even in her own town. Few things remained that she could recognize from childhood, despite the town politicians' effort to keep the area looking the way it had always been, with old-time Western wooden sidewalks and overhangs and wood and log storefronts. Sadly, their efforts hadn't succeeded.

Jackson had become a tourist town, a kind of prop. Six nights a week during summer, they staged a shoot-out on the town square. Actors carrying six-guns and shooting blanks robbed a stage. It was all mythological image-making, portraying Jackson as a Wild West town, which was not historically accurate. The nightly rodeo had been reduced to twice a week.

At one time, she liked the tourists and was proud to show off her lovely valley and its beautiful mountain ranges, forests and rivers. She loved the idea of being a "local." Actually, they lived a life independent of the tourists. It was also good when the tourists left and gave the locals back their town and their serenity.

Sometimes strangers would ask her how cold it got in winter and she would say, "Oh fifty degrees below or more."

They would wrap their hands around themselves in response, pucker their lips and say, "Brrrr." Of course, that was just a number. It never really felt that cold. In fact, it was lovely in winter, and the powdery snow made for wonderful skiing.

"I'd rather be poor as a church mouse here in this valley than rich anywhere else," she thought. Tears filled her eyes and spilled over her cheeks. "Please don't take me away, God," she begged aloud.

Driving north on Highway 89, she passed new buildings made to look old and new retail establishments and motels. There were few cars on the road and few signs of life. How many times had she headed north on this road to her parents home, built on the few remaining acres that the family had retained?

Gunning the motor, as if speed might assuage her frustration, she drove the few miles north to the Gros Ventre turnoff, then turned left and headed to the old ranch originally homesteaded by her family, now a posh subdivision and country club. Some of the houses were huge and easily would contain three the size of hers.

She saw the cottonwoods along the irrigation ditches that her grandfather had planted, now grown tall and sturdy. Beyond them, she could see the outlines of the mighty Tetons and the centerpiece of Jackson Hole, the Grand, reaching into the starry night sky nearly 14,000 feet high. Help me, she cried out to the Grand, which had watched over her from the moment she had seen the light of day.

She parked her car beside the road and began to walk through the land, meadows once grazed by cows but now given to sagebrush and high grass, yellowing in the late summer, no longer cut for hay. In the distance, she could see the sleeping hulks of the large new houses. Strangers were living on this land now, the land of her parents and grandparents. They were oblivious to the people who had lived here before.

As a child, she had walked these meadows. She had stood in the shade of the cottonwoods in summer and watched them silvery and leafless in winter. She had ridden her horses on this land, heard the cry of the ravens and the hawks who patrolled the skies and watched the sun rise over the Sleeping Indian and set over the Teton Range.

During winters, her father would transport her by horse-drawn sled from the ranch road to the highway. There, she would get on the school bus, not to return until dark. How she loved those cold dark winters, the family sitting before the fire, watching the dark clear night with its millions of stars.

Safe and cozy under her mother-made quilt she would hear the cry of the coyote in the night, and often in the morning would open her eyes to a herd of elk heading for the Elk Refuge. On other mornings, she would see a stray moose foraging in the snow.

The house they had lived in was long gone now and the road pattern had changed completely. She walked through the sagebrush to where the house once stood, an empty space now, surely on land that today would fetch more than the cumulative price three generations of her family had gotten for the land.

She walked around what she imagined was the perimeter of the old house, eyes down into the darkness, searching for some token, some errant belonging that might have been preserved accidentally when the house was bulldozed and the foundation buried in the earth. In her imagination, she summoned up the look of it, how it once stood, providing them all with a 360-degree view of the mountain ramparts.

It was a small log house with a picture window facing the Tetons, a second window looking out toward the Sleeping Indian and a third one overlooking the two Gros Ventre buttes in the background. No day went by without her seeing those sights, often taking them for granted. Those mountains are mine, she told herself. Why haven't they protected me?

To the east, she could see the first faint glow of the coming dawn. Soon the colors would begin their play of light, spilling over the mountain peaks, turning orange to yellow and every gradation between to signal the beginning of a new day. Then the ball of the sun would rise above the "Sleeping Indian" and suddenly light up the valley as if by a camera flashbulb.

She moved over familiar ground, certain she could remember each angle of each window of the old house. When she was sure, she stopped and spun around like a rotating top, remembering, feeling the sense of it and hearing the sound of wind as it whirled down the draw from the southwest.

"This was our place, Mama, Daddy, Grampa, Gramma. Why did you lose it?"

Suddenly, she fell to her knees and cried. Her shoulders shook with grief and sadness. She was not sure how long she kneeled there. She looked up at the sky where the twinkling stars were fading to make way for the rising sun. One more time, she told herself. One more time.

Her head rotated toward the sunrise, where the rim of the sun could be seen poking just above the peaks. Suddenly, kneeling there, she felt comforted by the sight. She did not feel as alone as she had felt before.

She got up and moved back to her car, then drove through the awakening town to the house that they had just sold. Parked in front was the moving van that Charlie had rented.

As she pulled up the driveway, her husband and children rushed out to greet and embrace her.

"The children were very worried, Alice," Charles said. "They wanted to call the sheriff."

"We were really scared, Mom," her thirteen-year-old daughter said as she joined in the embrace.

"They grow them strong out here in Jackson Hole," Charles said to his daughter. "Mom was just saying goodbye in her own way."

He was right, of course. Farewells were special and personal. And she knew that this place would never leave her heart, but the soul of her life was these people embracing her. This is her place, she told herself. It goes where I go.

# 4
# THE RAFTING TRIP

 Through the rearview mirror of the Ford Explorer,
Mary Hart could see Jim in the Chevy Suburban
hauling the trailer that carried the black raft, its
orange patches glistening in the bright sunlight of the wan-
ing September afternoon. He would follow her to the parking lot of the Grand Teton National Park headquarters, then
they would drive just beyond the Snake River overlook and
into the launching area.

She liked these late afternoon float trips and had packed
their usual rafting dinner of fried chicken, biscuits, coleslaw and brownies—and, of course, a wonderful vintage
bottle of Dom Perignon. As usual, they would beach the
boat on their favorite area along the bank and set out their
feast, drink the champagne and watch the sun lower itself
toward the peaks of the Teton Range.

This was the fifth summer they had spent in Jackson Hole,

in their house built on a high bench along Fall Creek Road. It was a large log house that they had designed and decorated, filling it with Western paintings and artifacts. Their three children were grown now and had families of their own. Those who had the time would spend a week with them, and they would plan wonderful side trips to keep children and grandchildren amused and interested.

Jim had come here as a boy to fly-fish with his dad, an avid fisherman, and their decision to build a home in Jackson Hole was not without its sentimental element of nostalgia for Jim.

"I've worked my ass off for thirty years for this moment," Jim had told her the very day they moved into their new house, which had taken two years to build. Mary knew, of course, that this had always been her husband's dream and was fully supportive of their decision to buy land and build this house.

Jim had made his money in the publishing business in New York. Mary had seen him through the struggle of the early years. In Jim's business life, she also was supportive, a true blue corporate wife who had done her fair share of entertaining and traveling with her husband, helping to solidify contacts and build the business.

They had an apartment on Fifth Avenue in Manhattan and Mary now devoted much of her time during the high social season raising money for various projects in the arts. She had many friends, and she and her husband were popular guests on the frenetic New York social circuit. For each of the past five years, they had spent July, August and part of September in Jackson, returning to New York in mid-September. During winters, they would come back for a week to ski and often would then spend another week or two in the warm climate of the Caribbean.

She liked the rhythm of their life-style, counting herself lucky to have the best of all worlds. In Jackson, Jim was something of an amateur naturalist. He loved fly-fishing, hiking and rafting. Although he once had devoted much recreational time to golf, he had eschewed the game for other activities connected with his naturalist leanings.

"When I get out here, Mary," he often told her, "I feel transformed, more alive."

She noted that during the past summer, he had been particularly absorbed in his naturalist activities, spending long hours taking nature hikes with people from the Park Service and attending lectures about the various aspects of the natural phenomena. At times, he would go off by himself, in good weather and bad, on what he called "nature" walks, equipped with binoculars and his books of birds and wildflowers. He had even bought himself a CD identifying bird songs and spent hours listening to these strange sounds.

She was only mildly interested in such things and occupied the times he was away by playing golf and bridge with her summer friends. Occasionally, she would join him on short morning treks and, gleefully, he would seek to identify every species he encountered. He could identify many birds by their bird songs, and it was not uncommon for them to stop and listen. He would raise his palm to signal quiet, then whisper the name of the bird.

Most of the birds he mentioned were ones she had rarely heard of, and though he would point out such exotic species as Western tanagers, golden-crowned kinglets or the great blue heron, she very often had to be reminded of their names. She could spot graceful trumpeter swans and did know the difference between elk and moose, and she was able to recognize such wildflowers as Indian paintbrush and yarrow, but her mind made no effort to commit such things to memory.

As a good corporate wife, she had been conditioned to "go along" with her husband's interests. It didn't take her long to understand that she really was not needed on these walks and, after awhile, she decided there was no point in joining him. She especially drew the line on overnight pack trips into the Teton Wilderness and Yellowstone.

During their first summer in Jackson Hole, they had taken a week-long pack trip into the Thorofare section of Yellowstone, one of the most remote areas of the wilderness. Between the long painful hours of riding into and out of the wilderness, the swarms of mosquitoes they had encountered, the distasteful pit latrines, the lack of bath facilities, the discomfort of sleeping bags and the fatty, high-cholesterol diet, she vowed never to do it again. And she hadn't.

Jim, on the other hand, loved pack trips and usually did one or more each summer without her. This summer, he had gone on two of them, each for four days, one in the Hoback area and one in the Teton Wilderness. On his return, he talked of his various adventures, and she had appeared to listen intently although secretly she had felt these recountings repetitive. She was thankful he hadn't pressed her to go with him.

"I'm so glad you had a great time," she told him when he returned from his trips.

"I think if you gave it more time and patience, you would have had a great time."

"I'm happy for you, Jim. It's just not my cup of tea."

By the third summer, he accepted the fact that she had no desire to join him and he made his plans accordingly. Jim seemed respectful and understanding about her distaste for horse-packing and her disinterest in his naturalist activities. She liked their occasional rafting trips, which were pleasant and not strenuous, and she did enjoy the picnic aspect of their evening river floats.

Mary's interest in the Jackson Hole area came from a different focus than her husband's: She liked the climate and the Western ambiance and she particularly enjoyed the house they had built and the views of the surrounding area, especially the mountains. She was supportive of his naturalist "hobbies", but in her heart, she did not share his enthusiasm for the outdoor life.

She was conscious of his many attempts to spark her interest in what he called "the natural glories" of the area, and she always listened intently for his sake, knowing that these forays to attract her to the subject would always end in her eventual indifference.

"Did you know," he asked her on numerous occasions, "that the wildlife outnumber the human population of Wyoming? Think of it. There are more elk, bison, moose, deer, pronghorn antelope, bighorn sheep, bears and dozens of smaller mammals than people."

"Fascinating."

"And most of it roams this northwest corner of the state. Do you realize that collectively our mountain ranges with their two national parks, five national forests, two national wildlife refuges and an Indian reservation constitute the largest wildlife preserve in the lower forty-eight?"

"Really."

The fact was that she was, body and soul, an urban Easterner, a dyed in the wool New Yorker. She loved city life more than the rugged Western country life, and although she tolerated her stays in Jackson Hole, she never could summon up the same passion for it as her husband. Yet, his well being and happiness had always been a priority in her life and the Jackson Hole experience was no exception. Mostly, she feigned contentment and, after a few weeks, began to count the days until she could return to Manhattan.

This probably would be the last raft trip they would take this season, which was fine with her. In a week, they would leave the caretaker in charge of the house and head home. To her, home was and always would be Manhattan. She had already filled her calendar with lunches, dinners, meetings and social events and was looking forward to them with happy expectation.

Jim, on the other hand, was showing signs of regret that the season was ending. He slowly had divested himself of the day-to-day routine of his business. With his telephone, computer and fax machine, he was able to communicate with his management and be available for the big decisions. She noted that he had spent less and less time in contact with his office this summer.

In fact, she had observed with passing interest that he rarely mentioned his business interests and seemed to spend more and more time on his naturalist bent. But then, during this latter part of his business career, he had rarely discussed business affairs with her anyway, even in New York.

Jim unfastened the raft from the flatbed, and he and Mary pushed it into the river using a tree to tie it in place before boarding. They fastened their life jackets, stowed their dinner on board, untied the hitch to the tree and jumped into the raft.

Planting himself upright in the rowing cockpit, Jim grasped the handles of the twelve-foot oars and maneuvered the raft into the center of the river's flow, which was always slower in September. By now, the Idaho farmers needed less water for their potato crops, and the Jackson Lake dam's output had slackened.

It was an exquisite afternoon. The air was crisp and clear, not a cloud visible in the cerulean sky. The raft meandered quietly downstream. On the steep eastern bank were stands of alpine and Douglas fir, and darting above them were rough-winged swallows. Occasionally, Jim would dip the oars, pulling on them to avoid the snags that always punctuated the river.

Mary sat facing her husband. She could tell that he was happy and confident, enjoying the process, alert to the feel of the river and its potential hazards. Jim had become quite proficient at guiding the raft safely through the water, and she did not feel any physical insecurity.

"There's an otter," he said with enthusiasm, pointing out the creature chirping away to announce his presence. She observed the animal with mild interest, wishing she could summon up the same sense of discovery and excitement as her husband had.

They moved softly downriver, Jim watching and listening. Suddenly, his arm shot up and he pointed to a bald eagle circling in the sky in its graceful glide, searching for prey.

"Isn't that the most wonderful sight to behold?" Jim asked.

They had always sighted at least one eagle on these trips, and it always amazed her how Jim seemed to feel that these sightings were some special new discovery.

"Wonderful," she commented, sensing, as always, that some comment was necessary to validate his enthusiasm.

They continued the journey downstream. There were no other rafting parties on the river. They were completely alone.

"A beaver," Jim said, pointing as a beaver slapped its tail on the surface of the water and disappeared.

"Feels like it belongs to us," Jim sighed, dipping the oars and pulling to avoid a snag. "It just doesn't get any better than this."

She smiled up at him and nodded. What could she say? He was enjoying some private ecstasy. The trip was nice and relaxing but hardly worthy of being the best that life had to offer. It struck her how far and deep the chasm was between their interests and, for the first time, she felt a strange sense of menace.

They were silent for a long time, then Jim headed the raft to the place where they would have their dinner. As they beached, Jim saw a mule deer and her fawns watching them from a stand of firs.

"Aren't they beautiful?" Jim asked, lifting the packs from the raft.

The deer had darted away too quickly for her to see them, but she acknowledged them anyway.

"Yes, they are," she answered.

They moved to a clearing beside a log that they used for seating and spread a tablecloth on the ground. Jim popped open the champagne and poured it into two plastic stem glasses, handing one to Mary.

"Here's to Manhattan," Mary said, lifting her stem glass. She was immediately sorry she had said that. Jim looked at her, hesitated and frowned. A shadow seemed to cross his face.

"Manhattan?" Jim said. "Here we are in God's country and you drink to that man-made jumble."

"It popped into my head. I guess I was thinking of going home," she said.

He drained his glass, then poured another without speaking. He seemed irritated, and his frown had deepened.

"This is my home," he said. "I hate Manhattan."

His comment was troubling. She studied his face and sipped the champagne, which seemed to her suddenly flat and tasteless.

"Hate Manhattan? When did this happen?" She felt the edge of panic begin.

"I've always hated it, Mary," he said.

"That's where your business is, Jim."

"I'm selling the business," he said.

"What?!" She was stunned.

"It doesn't interest me anymore."

"You always enjoyed the business. My God, you worked so hard to build it."

"I made all the money we'll ever need. The sale will bring us even more. Who cares? The kids'll get most of it, anyway." He waved his arm in an all-encompassing gesture. "What's money compared to this?"

She followed his gesture, feeling a knot building in her stomach.

"This? This means more than your business?"

"Infinitely more," he sighed. "This is my life, Mary. This is my place."

He took another sip of the champagne and shook his head.

"I'm not going back, Mary," he said. Their glances locked. She was not sure what he meant.

"Not going back?" she managed to say.

"My place is here," he said, lifting his arm once again. He looked toward the mountain range. "All this. The mountains, the rivers . . . everything. Life is a wink, Mary. I don't want us to go back."

"Us?"

"Of course, us."

"You mean live here all year-round? In winter?"

"The winters are wonderful," he said.

"Wonderful? It's like living in a freezer."

They were silent for a long time. She found herself trying to compose a proper response in her mind. His sudden announcement had taken her totally by surprise. She berated herself for not suspecting, for ignoring the many clues he had left.

He offered her more champagne, but she declined. Shrugging, he filled his own glass again.

"I just don't understand," she told him. "Are you saying that you intend to leave New York permanently?" Of course, she knew that was what he was saying, but it was so alien to her expectations that she couldn't believe it.

"That is my intention, Mary," he replied. "I hope I've made it clear. In this stage of our lives, New York has no point. We have a lovely house here with all the creature comforts. You'll get involved with the community as you have in Manhattan. Why on Earth must we live in a swirl of people and pollution? If it gets too uncomfortable, we could travel to a warm climate for a couple of weeks. And we could always visit in New York. Stay at a hotel, visit your friends. . . ."

"You mean give up our apartment?"

"No point in keeping it. Frankly, I'm ready to simplify our life, not complicate it. Why do we need more than one permanent residence?"

He drained the champagne from his glass and smiled. "We might as well put on the feedbag."

"You're serious," she said. "You're really serious."

"What's the big deal here, Mary? You look as if you just got news of the end of the world."

"I did, Jim. For me, it is the end of the world."

"Don't be ridiculous, Mary."

Without commenting, she opened the plastic bowls and doled out fried chicken, coleslaw and biscuits and handed him a paper plate and a plastic fork and knife. The sight of the food nauseated her and she put her own plate aside.

"I don't know if I can hack this, Jim," she said finally, still trying to assemble her thoughts into some coherence. "This is your place, not mine. I'm a city girl. I like it here, but I'm not as passionate about it as you are. Oh, I like to look at the birds and the animals and the wildflowers. They're very pretty. But that's about it. I love the tumult of Manhattan, the energy level, the rich cultural life. I love my friends there and can cope with the noise and the dirt. Oh, I enjoy the summers here. New York is not very nice in summer, hot, muggy, sticky. . . ." Suddenly she looked at him, her gaze meeting his. "Why aren't summers enough for you? Even most of the birds get out of the valley, the wildflowers die, the elk come down to the refuge, the bears hibernate and many of the humans leave. Why do you have to stay?"

She felt breathless from her long speech to which he had listened intently, nodding his head occasionally.

"Believe me, Mary, I do understand. I'm sorry. It was as if, as if I was a homing pigeon and had come to my home base. As you grow older, Mary, you begin to attach a lot more importance to place. In New York, lately, I feel like an alien. Not here."

She remained silent for a long time. She looked toward the river, but did not see it as something wonderful and soul-stirring. Rather, it seemed monotonous, relentless in its grey-green flow, a never-ending movement to nowhere. Turning her head, she gazed at the Tetons, still snowcapped after the long summer. She could see why other people could be moved by such a sight. To her, the mountains were repetitious, static, boring.

"Do you realize Jim, what you're asking me to do?" Mary sighed. She felt her world collapsing around her. To her mind, he had been brainwashed by the environment.

"Frankly, Mary, I don't see it as that much of a sacrifice. Why would anyone prefer to live elsewhere? Look around you, Mary. This is the real thing."

"Your real thing," she snapped. "Not mine." She felt the

beginnings of anger well up inside her. She had never felt such oncoming rage. It was as if an entire life of protest was rising up to consume her. She stood up.

At that moment, her gaze was deflected by something at the edge of the tree line. She turned to look. It was a moose and her calf, munching aspen branches. Jim followed her gaze.

"You can't see that in Manhattan," he whispered.

She did not reply. Instead, she moved a few steps toward the animals.

"What are you doing, Mary? You get too close to that calf, she'll charge you."

His words acted as a spur and she continued to move forward.

"Mary, you're being foolish. They're ornery. She gets it into her head you're after her calf, she'll go after you."

"Who cares?" she cried. "It would be just another natural phenomena. In your world, the animals have priority over humans anyway."

She felt unhinged, set adrift. What did danger matter now? Her life was on the verge of collapse anyway. Moving forward, she headed in the direction of the calf, who lifted its oddly angular head and observed her with dark limpid eyes. The mother moose turned to Mary and tensed.

"You'll get yourself trampled," Jim shouted.

She did not reply, conscious of her recklessness. At the very least, she thought, she was getting his attention. He must know to what lengths she would go to underline her position, to illustrate her defiance.

As she moved toward the calf, the mother moose charged toward her. At that moment, her fearlessness evaporated. The moose, in her ungainly way, moved swiftly. Mary could see the angry look in her eyes. Her instincts told her to run, but her legs remained firmly rooted to the ground.

Suddenly, Jim appeared between her and the charging moose. He was still carrying the champagne bottle, holding it by the neck as if it were a club. He whacked the moose a crashing blow on its snout, breaking the glass. Stunned, the moose stopped dead in its tracks.

"Let's get the hell out of here," Jim shouted, grabbing Mary's hand as they ran to the raft and jumped in. The moose remained stunned, shaking its massive head as if it might chase away the pain. The calf meandered over to its mother, oblivious to the events that had just occurred.

Jim quickly cast off and once again was in the cockpit, maneuvering the raft through the river channels, leaving their meal and utensils back at the clearing.

"Whatever got into you, Mary?" Jim asked as he headed the raft downstream. "You could have gotten killed."

Maybe she could have, she acknowledged to herself. But she sensed that she did not have the courage to be heroic or demanding. Jim had always set their agendas, and she was too conditioned to that fact to resist. It was her failing. Yet again, she knew she would surrender.

"First moose I ever saw launched like a ship," she said, hoping to dispel the crisis with humor. He chuckled lightly but his attention seemed elsewhere.

"I hope I didn't hurt her permanently," he said, shaking his head and pulling suddenly on the oars to avoid a snag.

Not her, Mary mumbled to herself. Not her.

She turned away from her husband's gaze, mostly to avoid him seeing her tears.

# 5
## CRIME AND PUNISHMENT

 About twice a month before the snows came, Sam Robbins took his mountain bike up Teton Pass and rode it over the pass from Wilson to Victor and back. The pass rises from the Wyoming side to the Idaho side nearly 11,000 feet over tight, dangerous switchbacks.

It is an awesome and strenuous trip for mountain bikers, and only the most hardy and athletic make the journey. Ten years ago, Sam Robbins had come to Jackson Hole from Tennessee, where he had attended the state university, majoring in physical education. He loved the outdoors and managed to make a decent living teaching skiing in winter and horseback riding in summer. During the shoulder months of October, November, March, April and May, when fewer tourists come, he taught exercise classes at the local health club.

Five years after coming to Jackson Hole, he fell in love

with Pam Barret and they married and had a child. People liked Sam Robbins. He was intelligent, friendly, good-natured and participated in community events. He rented a house south of town, and he and Pam were saving to build a house of their own on a one-acre lot that they had purchased in the area.

As a young happily married couple, Sam and Pam Robbins were popular and sought after as friends and companions. The only distinguishing characteristic that made the Robbins' appear different from the others was the fact that Sam Robbins was black and Pam was white.

Sam Robbins was not naive. He knew even before he arrived in Jackson Hole that it had few, if any, blacks. In fact, when he settled in the valley, he discovered that he was the only visible black person in Jackson Hole. He did hear that there was one or two black ranchers around Pinedale but he never met them.

His mother had warned him that going to a place where there were no black people would expose him to discrimination and, perhaps, danger.

"Wyoming is cowboy country and cowboys carry guns," she argued to buttress her warnings.

"That's movie stuff," he countered. "In fact, Mama, most of the early cowboys were blacks and Mexicans." This was a fact he had learned from his black-history class in college.

"Are any of them left?" Sam's mother had inquired, implying that they had been eliminated by either lynching or banishment.

"People are people, Mama," he told her, understanding her concern. She was a churchgoing, God-fearing woman, but she had lived in an era of terrible prejudice and believed in her heart that white people, regardless of the laws they passed against discrimination, hated black people.

"Black folks and white folks are oil and water, son," she told him. Sam loved his mother dearly and was tolerant of her paranoia. She was of a different generation, and her judgment was warped by the terrible injustices through which she had lived.

Although Sam Robbins knew the art of living defensively—the natural instincts of any minority—he encountered no overt presence of racial discrimination in Jackson Hole. Not that he looked for it or wore his color on his sleeve. He was inescapably black, referring to himself in self-deprecating humor as "black as the ace of spades."

In the valley of Jackson Hole, there were a handful of Native Americans, descendents of the Shoshone, Gros Ventre or Blackfeet tribes that once used the valley as summer hunting grounds. Most of them appeared indigenous, hardly recognizable as different. There also was a small community of Mexicans, many of them illegals from the same town in Mexico, but the language barrier made them cluster together in tiny barrios in Jackson or over the pass in Idaho. That was the extent of the minority population.

Despite his color, Sam felt a sense of inclusion and acceptance. He liked people and they liked him. He judged people solely on their behavior and hoped that others did likewise. His mother's warnings notwithstanding, it did not take him long to feel free and equal in Jackson Hole. After all, people told him, this was the Equality State and the town of Jackson actually elected the first all-women town council in American history.

"We're Westerners," the old-timers would tell him. "A man's character is what counts." It was exactly what Martin Luther King had preached and he felt happy and comfortable living among people who felt the same way as he and Dr. King.

Sometimes people joked about him as being Jackson's "black minority" but this was presented with good humor and he was not offended by it. Pam, on the other hand, was more sensitive to such remarks.

"Where there's smoke, there's fire," she told him.

"You sound just like Mama."

As the years passed, he felt that he and Pam were part of the community, with the same concerns that other couples of their age were experiencing—higher taxes, the cost of housing and the quality of the area's schools, for example.

"That's the price we pay for living in paradise," Sam said often. This was the mantra of the working people in Jackson Hole. They had to make sacrifices to live in Paradise.

One day in April, Sam took his bike over the pass. The weather was brisk and he enjoyed the chill on his face as he cycled up from the Wyoming side, then coasted down toward Idaho. He loved the challenge of the pass, the hard peddling up and the controlled speed required on the downhill slope. Often, people waved as they passed him and he, as is traditional in Wyoming, acknowledged their greeting.

It was mid-afternoon, a time he often chose, because there would be less traffic on the pass. As he pounded the pedals upward, returning home from the Idaho side, he was conscious of a movement behind him. This was unusual since most times he would drive far to the right to make room for passing cars.

Looking back, he noticed a pickup directly on his tail. He caught only the briefest glimpse of the driver and his companion in the front seat. When the truck persisted, he waved it on, but it didn't respond. He wasn't quite sure whether or not this was an act of harassment. Bikers were sometimes hassled by impatient drivers, but, in this instance, he was far enough over to the right that it shouldn't have made any difference in the truck's ability to pass.

Steeling himself, he concentrated on the upward climb. On one of the first switchbacks, the truck's horn blared, then banged out some semblance of a rhythm. It was unnerving, but Sam did not look back. Just some drunken rednecks harassing a biker, he told himself, trying to ignore the grating sounds of the horn. Then suddenly it stopped. Sam was encouraged. Perhaps they were tiring of their so-called fun.

Then the motor gunned behind him and the truck pulled up beside him, slowing down to match the pace of the bike.

"Hey, monkey," one of the men called out. He was the passenger.

Sam deliberately ignored the man.

"Hey, monkey, monkey, monkey," the man cried. "Wanna banana?"

Sam saw a banana peel fall in front of his bike. Only then did he turn to look at the man harassing him. The man had long unruly hair and the look of a red-neck. Sam figured he was drunk. The man was howling with laughter.

Then the man on the driver's side perched over the passenger and called out.

"Ridem monkey man. Ridem. Dumb monkey fuck."

The pickup moved closer to Sam's bike.

"Hey monkey asshole. Get outta the way."

The horn blared and the men continued to laugh.

"Don't be crazy," Sam shouted to them as the pickup came dangerously close to him.

"Monkey talks. Ever see a monkey talk?"

Up ahead, Sam saw the crest of the pass. He pushed harder. Still, there were no other vehicles in sight. Suddenly, the pickup pulled away, then moved in front of the bike.

The man beside the driver stretched his head out of the window and shouted.

"No monkeys allowed on the pass. All monkeys go home to the jungle."

Sam noted that the vehicle had Wyoming plates. He memorized the numbers. Suddenly the truck slowed, then picked up speed, blowing exhaust in Sam's face. Relieved by their departure, he pushed hard to gain the crest. He was angry, of course, but calmer now that the truck was out of sight. As much as he wanted to deny it, he could not escape the conclusion that the remarks were meant to be racial slurs.

He figured the men were high and just playing around. At least, he hoped so. He had never experienced this kind of insult, and he assuaged his anger by believing these were just a couple of good old boys blowing off some steam. He hoped that they had gotten bored with harassment and driven on.

Reaching the crest of the pass, he started to switch gears when he felt himself pushed from the side, losing his balance on the bike. He fell hard on the asphalt and the two men picked him up roughly and pushed the bike to a side of the road. Sam noted the smell of sweat and alcohol as the men manhandled him to the road that led up to the ridgeline.

There they had parked the pickup. Out of sight of the pass road, they tied Sam's hands behind him and pushed him into the front seat of the pickup.

"You fellas have no right to do this," Sam managed to say. He was scared. The men were rough types. They wore tight jeans, cowboy boots, white T-shirts and leather belts with silver cowboy buckles. Sam noted some papers on the floor of the pickup with the name of a construction company on its masthead. He memorized the name: "Valley Construction."

"Monkey says we have no rights," the driver said. He was balding, and his hair was dirty and scraggly. He needed a shave. The other one was younger, probably still in his teens.

"Just taking you back in the jungle where you belong," the younger one said.

"Let's hear some monkey talk, monkey."

Sam felt a hard pinch on his arm and let out a scream of pain.

"Monkey talks funny," the driver said.

He drove the truck upward and parked it where it couldn't be seen from the pass road. Then they manhandled Sam out of the truck.

"What'll we do with the monkey?" the driver asked. He drew out a can of beer from under the seat and drank a deep swallow, then handed it to the younger man.

"Do monkey's dance?" the driver asked.

"You heard the man, monkey," the teenager said. "Do monkey's dance?"

"This is going too far, boys," Sam said, trying desperately to keep calm. His hands were tied solid and he felt helpless.

"Hell, we can go further than that, can't we, boy?" the older man said.

"Better believe it," the teenager said. He opened the pickup and took a hunting knife from out of the glove compartment.

Sam tried backing away, but the older one jerked the end of the rope and Sam lost his balance and fell to the ground.

"What do you say we strip the monkey?" the older man said. "I ain't seen no monkeys wearing clothes."

They kneeled beside Sam. The teenager sliced away his biker's jacket and tried to pull off his pants. At that point,

Sam kicked away with his feet, catching the older man in the thigh, knocking him over.

"Monkey likes to fight," the teenager said, straddling Sam across the stomach and holding the flat blade of the knife to his throat.

The older man lifted himself off the ground and came forward to where the teenager was straddling Sam. Suddenly, their eyes met and, for the first time since the episode began, he caught a note of hesitation in the man's expression.

"What do you say, we off this monkey. Maybe let the bears get him. Don't bears like monkey meat?" the younger man said.

"Rather see the monkey dance," the older man said.

Sam still felt the cold blade of the knife at his throat. He kept himself stock still. He had no experience in handling these circumstances.

"Maybe we cut his balls off, he can't make no more monkeys," the younger man said. With his free hand, he grabbed Sam's genitals.

"I'd rather see him do his monkey dance," the older man said. Sam could tell that the man was beginning to see that the situation had gone too far.

"I say we cut his balls off," the younger man said, "stuff em in his mouth."

"Jesus, Roy," the older man said.

Sam said nothing, hoping that the older man might realize that it had gone over the top.

"Never seen no monkey balls," the teenager said, pulling at Sam's underwear with his free hand while still holding the flat side of the knife to his throat. Sam closed his eyes. He was pinned down by the husky younger man and couldn't move.

"You scared, man?" the younger man asked Sam. He had spat out the question and Sam felt his saliva on his face. Sam nodded.

"Yeah, I'm scared. I got a wife and kid."

"Monkey has a wife and kid," the younger man said, howling. "One widow and orphan comin' up."

"Let's get on back," the older man said suddenly.

"You chicken, man?" the younger man said.

"Let's get on home," the older man said. He seemed concerned now.

"I'd do it, too," the younger man said. "Cut 'em right off."

"Sure you would, Roy."

"Stuff em in his mouth."

"I know that, Roy."

The younger man looked down at Sam and grinned.

"No, I wouldn't," he said. "Just seeing how scared monkeys can get. Bet he shit his pants."

The younger man got off Sam and put the knife in his belt.

"You had me scared too," the older man said to the younger one, the one named Roy.

"I was only havin' fun," the younger man said.

"He wouldn't hurt a fly," the older man said, addressing himself to Sam who was still lying on the ground.

"We was just having fun," the younger man said.

The older man lifted Sam to a standing position, and the younger one cut the rope from his hands.

"We didn't mean no harm," the older man said. "We was just playin' around."

Sam said nothing. Common sense told him to stay calm, keep his mouth shut.

"Smart thing would be just to keep this between us," the older man said.

Sam did not respond. He found his pants and put them on. It was beginning to get dark.

"Hope you can take a joke," the older man said. "I mean I got a wife and kid, too. And this boy comes from a good family."

"We wuz only playin' around," the younger man said. "We did you no harm."

Sam still said nothing. There was no point. If he spoke, he knew, he would show them his anger.

"You get my drift, then?" the older man asked.

"He ain't gonna do nothin'," the younger one said, touching the handle of his knife, his threat implicit in the action.

"Just jokin'. We can give you a lift to the road."

"It's OK," Sam said. "It's not far."

"No," the older man said. "We gotta give you a lift. See if the bike's OK."

Reluctantly, Sam got into the pickup. Still, he said nothing. He felt nauseated by the smell of the men and the residue of his own fear. He had been scared, but he had hated his being scared, almost as much as he hated the two men. He needed to get away from them as quickly as he could. They drove him to the pass road and the older man got out and picked up the bike.

"Looks OK to me," he said.

"Looks just fine," the younger man said.

Sam got out of the truck and inspected the bike. It seemed to be in working order and he could coast down the pass to where he had parked his car at the bottom of the old pass road.

"You gonna be OK, man?" the older man asked.

Sam nodded.

"We don't want no trouble," the older man said.

"Hell, no," the younger one said. "We was just playing. Maybe had one too many."

"No maybes. We did have one too many."

The men laughed and got into the pickup.

"Remember what we said," the older man said. He did not wait for a response, but gunned the motor and headed down the pass. Sam mounted his bike and started coasting down the road. Tears were rolling out of his eyes, down his cheeks. His nose ran and he wiped the mucous and tears away with the back of his hand.

For the first time since he had come to Jackson Hole, he felt like a black man. And yet the terrible men who had tortured and abused him had not once used the term "nigger."

When he got home, he took a long hot shower, scrubbing himself as if to wash away the horror of the experience, the cruel words, the violence and threats. When he finally was able to communicate rationally with Pam, he told her the story.

"Are you going to let them get away with it, Sam?" Pam asked.

"Will the punishment fit the crime?" Sam asked. He had been contemplating all aspects of revenge. They had abused him, insulted him, humiliated him, threatened him and his family. And for no other reason than that he was different. They called him a monkey. He was sickened by his own role. Had he been too frightened to fight back with all his strength? Did they really believe he would be docile enough to let the matter rest? They didn't seem too worried about him going to the authorities.

He pondered whether or not he should call attention to himself, a black man, and force people to discuss the matter, perhaps take sides. What he worried about most of all was that people actually might believe that this was nothing more than a prank, a game played by people who were a little high on alcohol. Some would wonder if calling him a monkey could really be considered a racial epithet. Would people think he was embellishing the story? The two men, however horrible they treated him, were obviously working people doing hard labor. Their pickup truck coughed and sputtered and the body work was chipped and dented and the paint job almost totally faded.

"They also threatened you and little Sam."

"I'm not afraid."

"I am!" he shot back angrily.

He did promise her that he would turn it over in his mind and try to figure out the best course of action. He knew what his mother would say. Ignore those terrible whites. Their souls will not rise up to meet the Lord. She would also rebuke him yet again for living in that strange white land instead of in the bosom of his own people. She did not approve of his marriage to Pam, although little Sam spent weeks at a time with his grandmother, who loved him dearly despite the lightness of his skin.

After a sleepless night, Sam got out of bed the next morning and announced his decision. He was going to tell the sheriff. He had the license-plate number on the pickup memorized and he also remembered the name of the company with which they probably were associated. Surely, with his sworn testimony, the sheriff would understand that a heinous crime had been committed. The question in Sam's mind was the punishment. In his mind, that punishment had to be equal to the crime.

He told his story to the sheriff, who expressed his anger and rage.

"Not on my turf," he fumed, taking notes furiously. "This is Wyoming."

He called two of his men into his office and gave them the details, and in a few moments they came back with the information needed. They had the owner of the pickup, a man named Larsen who lived in a trailer on Gregory Lane.

Within an hour, both men stood, sheepishly, handcuffed together in the sheriff's office. Sam was present.

"These them?" the sheriff asked.

Sam looked at the men who could not look him in the eye. The older man was ashen and the younger looked grim and frightened.

"I got a wife and kid," Larsen said. He was the older man. "We didn't mean no harm. Did we, Roy?"

Roy shook his head and looked downward.

"You accosted this man, roughed him up, called him vile names and threatened to cut off his genitals. Is that true?"

Roy nodded, shuffled his feet and looked at the ground.

"We did him no harm," the older man said. "We had one too many is all."

"How would you like someone to do to you what you did to this man?" the sheriff asked. Both men continued to look at the ground.

"He says you threatened him with more violence if he reported this crime?" He pointed to the knife they had taken from the younger man. "This your weapon, Roy?"

Roy nodded in the affirmative. Sam looked at the knife and shuddered.

"Do a little castrating with that, would you Roy?"

"I wouldna done nothin'," he whispered.

"I could give this knife here to Sam. See what he would do with it. Would you like that?"

The man shook his head.

"Well we got the ID," the sheriff said. "We'll see what we can do to throw the book at them."

"Isn't there somethin' we could do?" the older man said with a quavering voice. "We got drunk is all, went nuts. We didn't mean no harm."

He lifted his head and looked at Sam.

"I'm sorry man, really sorry. We got nothin' against you or your kind. It was wrong." His voice trailed off. Sam said nothing.

"Nothing against his kind?" the sheriff said. "You called him a monkey. What is that supposed to mean?"

"We got nothin' against black people," the older man said. "Live and let live."

"But you didn't," the sheriff pressed.

"We was drunk," the older man mumbled, looking at his shoes. Sam thought he looked pathetic.

"Don't look so tough now," the sheriff said.

"Look, I got a wife and kid," the older man pleaded, looking at Sam. "Tell them to give us a break."

"We're going to do just that. Give you three squares and a roof over your head, courtesy of the state. Maybe even the feds will take a look. Say bye-bye to the wife and kid, you scumbags."

Instead of relief, Sam felt anguished. In his heart, he wanted these men punished, wanted his revenge, wanted them to feel the same psychic pain he had experienced. On the other hand, he felt compassion for the family of the older man, especially his wife and child.

"We'll call you when we need you, Sam," the sheriff said.

"What will happen to them?" Sam asked.

"Lawyer will get them bail and they'll probably get some time. At least I hope so. Terrible thing they did to you, Sam."

Sam continued to be troubled. All that day, he couldn't eat and at night he tossed in his bed unable to sleep.

"What is it, Sam?" Pam asked.

"The punishment must fit the crime," he muttered.

"You don't make or administer the laws, Sam. Just hope they get what they deserve."

Her remark seemed to stimulate his thinking and some-time toward morning he got his idea.

When the prosecuting attorney arrived at work that day, Sam was waiting for him at the door. By then, the story of Sam's agony had gone through town like brushfire. He had no doubt that he would be contacted by reporters from the *Guide* and the *News* and the radio stations. He hated the idea of being the center of attention, especially on the basis of race. He had never wanted to be singled out for that reason alone. Unfortunately, there was no way to avoid it.

The prosecuting attorney was sympathetic and gracious. He also was appalled at what the two men had done to Sam and assured him that they would be prosecuted to the full extent of the law. He cited a number of statutes that had been criminally violated—not to mention Federal Civil Rights violations.

"I have a better idea," he told the prosecuting attorney, proceeding to outline what he had in mind in greater detail.

"I don't know if it would pass muster," the prosecuting attorney countered. "Might get the ACLU up our gazoo. Although . . ." He suddenly became thoughtful.

"Suppose we got the men's consent?" Sam asked.

"Make a deal?"

"A signed consent to participate," Sam said. "They would be doing it voluntarily. Better than time."

"Send a helluva message," the prosecuting attorney said. "I love it. But I'm going to have to speak to the judge and the lawyer for the defendant."

"I think I can persuade them," Sam said.

"You?"

"Hell," Sam said. "I'm the victim. I think they'll listen."

Late that afternoon, the prosecuting attorney called Sam's home.

"Got a go for your idea, Sam. Depends on both defendants' written consent. Doesn't mean we won't be sued but we're all willing to take the chance."

"And my meeting with them?"

"Arranged," the prosecuting attorney said.

That evening, Sam went down to the sheriff's office and the two prisoners were taken to a room with a table. The three men sat around the table while one of the sheriff's men looked on. As before, the men were downcast and nervous.

"We did a terrible thing to you, Mr. Robbins," said Larsen, the older man.

"I was the worst," the younger man said. "I don't have nothin' against you for being a black man. Hell, I don't even know any black men."

"I've got a wife and kid," Larsen said. "Same as you."

"I'm not impressed by your show of remorse, gentlemen," Sam said. "What you did to me deserves the hardest punishment the law allows. Put yourself in my shoes."

"It's the alcohol made me crazy, Mr. Robbins," the younger man said. "I can't believe I got so crazy."

"Don't blame the alcohol," Sam said. "Something mean inside both of you made you do this to me. The truth is I hate both of you for what you did. But I do have this idea. It needs your written consent. And if you do it, you may not have to serve time, but I can't guarantee that."

The two men exchanged glances, then listened raptly as Sam outlined his plan.

"Jeez," Larsen said, rubbing his chin. "My kid'll see it.

All my friends and the guys that work with me. . . ." His voice trailed off.

"Better than time," Sam said. "Besides, it's sure to be in the papers anyway."

"Lawyer said we may get off," Roy said. "Though I did get that DUI last year."

"I never been in trouble with the law," the older man said.

"That's the deal. Take it or leave it," Sam said. "I've got all the permissions I need."

The men exchanged glances again.

"You said in writing," Larsen said.

"I've prepared a document for both of you to sign," Sam said. He handed the two-page document to Larsen and both men read it carefully.

"Says we were malicious, cruel, unfeeling, insensitive and violent." There was no mention of the men being drunk, which was deliberate. Sam did not believe that alcohol was to blame. It simply lit the spark to already dry tinder. Larsen continued to read, then shook his head and looked up at Sam.

"Makes us seem like a couple of animals."

"Beasts," Sam said. "Beasts in the jungle."

"I was the real bad one," Roy said. "Larsen's got a family. Maybe you can sort of let him out of it."

"Both," Sam said. "It's true, you were the worst. But Larsen went along. People who do that are just as guilty as the others."

"Any way my kid don't have to see this?" Larsen asked.

"Mine will," Sam said. "Yours should."

"How would you like it?" Larsen said. "See his father like that."

"How would my son have reacted?" Sam said. "Seeing you do what you did to his father?"

"Shit," Larsen said. "I'll sign. Better than prison."

"Me, too," Roy said.

The sheriff's man went out of the room to get a notary. While he was gone, Sam spoke to the two men.

"Why?" he asked them.

Larsen looked at his hands, then up into the face of the younger man.

"I don't understand it. Maybe because you were different than me, than us. You know, a different color. Fact is, I don't have no prejudice in my heart. We was just being damned fools."

"Maybe I been lookin' at too many bad movies," the younger man said. "Maybe we were just angry and you came across our path."

"Angry at me?" Sam asked.

"Maybe bein' angry bein' what we are," Roy said. "Workin' stiffs. Bottom-of-the-barrel boys. Maybe that."

"Even so," Sam said. "Why me?"

"I don't like what I did," Larsen said, shaking his head. "I don't even know where the idea came from." He paused. Tears filled his eyes. "Are we evil men, Mr. Robbins?"

"You are to me," Sam said, getting up from the table. He felt a sudden surge of compassion, which he didn't want to feel. A notary came in and watched the men sign the document, then put her stamp on it. The sheriff's man took the documents and put the cuffs back on the two men, and Sam left the room.

The wooden cage was set up in the Town Square, and the two men were placed in it on Saturday morning. Inside the cage was a curtained-off area and a portable toilet. There was hay on the floor, but not a stick of furniture in the cage. Over the cage was a sign "Beware: Savage Beasts."

The local newspapers put out a special edition announcing the event, and the radio and television stations donated time for the announcement. Not everybody was pleased by the idea, of course. Nevertheless, most of the locals and some tourists joined the lines of people viewing the two men.

Most of the time, the men sat on the floor cross-legged, their heads bowed. No one really knew how to react to the spectacle. Some were simply silent. Others cursed the men, pouring invective on them for disgracing the town. Occasionally, one or the other of the men would look up at the passing parade of people and remark: "We were wrong to do what we did. But we are not evil men."

Sam came early before the crowds. He brought Pam with him, and little Sam. While he had enjoyed the idea when it was an abstraction, the reality sickened him. He was sorry he had put it in motion and, although he still despised the men for what they had done to him, he could not dismiss the great swell of compassion that rolled over him. They were, after all, human beings just like him.

"I didn't want this," he told the men through the bars of the wooden cage.

"Either did we," Larsen said. "Sittin' here, I'm wondering if hard time isn't better."

"I'd rather be here," the younger man said.

"Are they bad people, Daddy?" little Sam asked. He had not told the boy what the men had done to him.

"Very bad," Pam said.

"They did a bad thing, but they're not bad people," Sam said. He was surprised by his own statement.

"Let's go home," he said and as he turned he saw another woman holding the hand of a child about little Sam's age.

"It's OK, Hank, we still love you," the woman said. Her

eyes were red with tears and the little boy stared at his father through the bars, uncomprehending.

"We did a bad thing to that man," Larsen said, pointing with his chin. The woman turned and stared at Sam's black face. Sam imagined he could see the hatred in her eyes.

"Two wrongs don't make a right," she said.

Sam felt his stomach lurch. He turned away from the woman and walked with Pam and little Sam back to his car.

"They deserved it," Pam said as he drove home.

"The punishment fit the crime." Sam said, adding after a long silence "Didn't it?"

# 6
# A DOWNHILL STORY

Rendezvous Mountain in Jackson Hole represents the longest continual vertical drop of any ski resort in the United States. It attracts skiers from all parts of the world who like the challenge of the steep run and are willing to forego the state-of-the-art amenities offered at other resorts.

They were sitting near the big window of the ski cafeteria sipping cocoa. The sun soon would perch itself on the highest peak, then, in less than a couple of minutes from the time the lowest edge of the diameter hit the peak, it would disappear and the temperature would drop a good ten degrees.

But neither the young man nor the young woman was thinking about that. The young man, whose name was Bert Harper, looked intense and anxious, and the young girl, Sally Forman, looked troubled and sad.

The ski resort would be closing in a few days and Bert's job with the ski school would be over. Sally, who was not with the ski school, but was an expert skier, was expected back in Boston tomorrow to begin a good high-paying job with a software firm.

She had taken a year off after graduation and had bummed around Europe and the States for almost a year, then had landed in Jackson Hole and fallen in love with the young man. They loved each other intensely, convinced that their love was stronger than any that had ever happened in the world before. It was, they told each other, the most profound magical relationship that two people could ever have.

"The most important thing is that we love each other," Bert said. He had been saying the same thing in various creative ways for weeks now. He had not been able to talk the girl out of leaving Jackson Hole. "That's numero uno right?"

"Right."

"But not enough for you to stay here with me?"

"You know that's not true."

"It is true. Otherwise, you'd stay."

"There's no future here, Bert. After the ski resort closes, we'll be scratching to make ends meet."

"I'm lined up as a waiter in town, and in the summer I can wrangle horses at the dude ranches."

"Where's the future in that?" the girl asked.

She had been sharing quarters with him in a tiny apartment at the south end of town. They had met in December and it now was the middle of March. It was, as they say, love at first sight. After skiing, making love was their highest priority. Food and sleep were far, far down the list. They could not get enough of each other.

"We have broken the world's record for lovemaking," Bert insisted.

"If you'd have given me one dollar each time, I'd be a multimillionaire," Sally joked. They always laughed a lot together.

"Why are you so worried about the future?" Bert asked. "For us, the future is now. There's plenty of time to worry about that other future, the scary one."

"The point is that if we don't get started on something, others will take our place and we'll fall behind, then we won't get anywhere."

"Where is there to get? Look around you. This is the place. Look at the mountain and the sky. Where else in the world will you find that? We love each other and we're in the most beautiful place in the world. It won't ever get any better than this."

"It is beautiful here, Bert. And you're probably right, it won't ever get better than this."

"So where's the argument? Admit it. Have you ever felt more alive than this, anyplace, in your whole life?"

"Never," Sally said. She picked up her cocoa, found it cold, then put the mug back on the table.

The red tram passed overhead and she watched for a moment as it sailed through the sky to the top of Rendezvous Mountain. The sun hit the peak and started downward. Soon it would get colder, attracting those who liked their late runs, when the slopes were less crowded.

"You can't leave Sally," Bert said, after the tram had passed. "You mustn't leave."

"Then you come with me. Boston is not a bad place. Boston is great."

"I've been there. I've been all over. This is the only place. Here I stay."

"You're a stubborn fool."

"Once I go away, the next thing you know I'll get ambition, find a high-paying job, become a city person. I did that. I felt like a mouse on a treadmill. That's not a life. A living death, that's what it is. I've made my choice."

"You're a chemical engineer with a master's degree. You can get a job anywhere."

"That's all in the past. I liked the science but I hated the structured life. Engineers are boring, too anal, too small. Working as an engineer I felt like a prisoner. Here I feel free and happy. And I have you." He took her hand and kissed each finger, then sucked her left forefinger as if it were candy.

"You can visit," the girl said.

The fact was that her heart was breaking. She did not want to go, but she was too afraid to stay, too afraid that she would love it here and become a kind of drifter like Bert and scratch for a living, then find herself older and left out. She was deeply frightened of that. Her parents, whom she adored and who had financed her year off, would think she had lost her mind. She was an only child and they had high hopes for her.

"What is the most powerful thing in the world?" Bert asked.

"You never give up," she said.

"Answer the question," Bert insisted, still sucking her finger.

"Love. Love is the most powerful thing in the world."

"If you really believed that, you would stay."

"Bert, stop whipping yourself. We've been through that."

"Stay, Sally. Stay. Stay."

"You're killing me, Bert."

She felt sick at heart, unsure, and she had projected what it would mean to wake up without him, not to hear his voice, not to make love to him, to yearn for him. It was an awful, empty feeling.

But she also had projected another possibility, their growing older, still scratching for a living, priced out, struggling, holding two jobs, being exhausted, being servants to richer people. That wasn't freedom. She hated these thoughts, hated the ring of truth in them.

The sunlight was fading now and the electric lights seemed brighter as the darkness descended. You could tell from the vapor coming out of the people's mouths who were finishing their runs that the temperature had dropped. The snow looked pure white, like whipped cream, and the lines of electric lights made the ski area look like a Swiss Village.

"You know, of course, that my heart is breaking," Bert said.

"So is mine."

"Breaking into 10,000 pieces, exploding."

"Mine, too. Twenty thousand pieces."

"Then stay. Why should your heart explode into 20,000 pieces? I love you. I need you. I long for you. Feel how much."

He took the finger he was sucking and brought it and the hand under the table to feel his erection.

"Is that love or merely sexual attraction?" she asked.

"When it goes together, it is something rare and wonderful and special. It is the way a man's body speaks the truth."

"A man's heart is not there."

"Mine is. It is the barometer of my longing for you."

"I know. A woman has signs too."

"Don't go, my love, my sweet love, my Sally."

"You're making me crazy," the girl said. "It's not fair."

"Life is unfair. But this is fair. This is the fairest thing there is."

They paused to watch the tram descend, then they looked at each other. Sally saw him through tear-glazed eyes.

"I wish I was two people. One who went and one who stayed."

"How will I get through the days without you?" Bert sighed. She could tell he was beginning the process of acceptance. Now she projected other thoughts. After her would come other girls. He had needs. He was very emotional and giving. A pang of jealousy charged through her.

"What's to become of you, Bert?"

"I was thinking the same thing about you. One thing I know for sure is that it will never be like this, not ever."

She turned away, knowing in her heart that he was right. Tears spilled over her eyelids and slid down her cheeks.

"Stay, Sally," Bert whispered. It was, she knew, his last gasp of persuasion. His eyes were also filled with tears.

"I can't," she whimpered.

"You'll never come back to me. You'll get caught up in your job and other people. You'll join the achievers out there. You'll be successful and marry some rich successful guy and have babies who will grow up to be achievers."

"Stop that. Please stop that."

"All right, I'll stop."

They were silent for awhile.

"We could take one last run together," Bert said.

"I'd like that."

Bert paid the girl at the register for the cocoa.

"Hi, Bert," the girl said, smiling. Sally also smiled, but it was false. Suddenly, she ached with jealousy.

"That's Geraldine," Bert said. She has her master's in psychology. You don't see her complaining."

"She will," Sally said, still seething with jealousy, imagining Bert and Geraldine hitting it off, going to bed together.

They got their skis off the rack and waited for the tram to descend. They stood close together and kissed.

"I love you, my sweet, dearest, most wonderful love."

"I love you more."

"Me more."

Behind them, someone giggled and said: "Ain't love grand?"

Bert recognized someone he had taught at the ski school.

"Better than a kick in the head," Bert said, smiling and continuing to kiss Sally.

The tram came and they went in and stood close together, still kissing as it ascended and, in ten minutes, reached the top of Rendezvous Mountain. They got out of the tram and slipped into their skis and stood at the very tip of the slope, looking out over the valley. To the east, they could see the outlines of the Gros Ventre mountain range.

The valley floor was a glistening white carpet. In the distance, they could see puffs of smoke from the fireplaces of the houses, and the lights of the village were bright and cheerful.

"This is it," Bert said, looking out over the valley.

"Yes, it is," Sally agreed.

"I said *it*," Bert said, "meaning all-encompassing, the ultimate best."

"I can't argue with you, Bert."

"Then stay."

"Please, Bert."

They put on their ski goggles and dug their sticks into the snow.

"A straight run, as fast as we can go." Bert said.

"Be careful."

"What for? . . ." Bert began pushing off, his voice disappearing in the swish his skis made. She pushed off behind him, jumped off a mogul, then followed, gaining speed. He was crouched low, ski poles tight against his elbows at right angles to his body.

He was descending in a straight line, moving faster than she had ever seen him go, and it suddenly struck her that he was being very reckless, traveling at a dangerous speed on snow that was icing up fast. Her heart began to pound with fear, and although she also was descending fast, she was angling, putting a more cautious brake on her speed.

There was still enough light to keep him in view and, even before she saw him crash, she knew that he would, that that had been his intention all along, that he was showing her that his life meant nothing without her and that it was all her fault.

He had lost control on an ice patch, whipsawed, then went sideways, shoulder over shoulder for maybe 100 yards, losing his skis, which hurtled downward in opposite directions on their own. She watched him turn and toss in the air like a paper caught in an eddy of hard breeze and heard herself scream.

"What have you done, Bert? What have you done?" she cried to herself as she sped downward, angling sharply to a stop near his body. She kicked off her skis and crouched beside him, searching his face for signs of life, but knowing that she must not move his body for fear of making things worse.

"Bert, my love. Oh Bert. What have you done?"

He was still breathing but he was obviously unconscious. She could not tell how badly he was injured. Thankfully, someone from the ski patrol had seen the accident and was there within minutes, summoning help on his radio.

"Jeez, it's Bert," the ski patroller said, bending over Bert's inert body. "Looks bad."

"It's my fault," Sally said. "My fault."

"Your fault?" the ski patrol guy said. "I saw the whole thing. You weren't even near him."

They were quick to bring a stretcher, and three ski patrollers very carefully put him on it and skied him slowly down the slope with Sally following, sobbing and slightly hysterical, blaming herself for all that had happened.

In the ambulance, the attendant gave Bert a shot and checked his vital signs, while Sally crouched next to Bert on the stretcher and stroked his hand.

"I'm sorry, Bert, so sorry. Forgive me, my love. Can you ever forgive me?"

The attendant looked at her and put his hand on her shoulder. The fellow from the ski patrol who had witnessed the accident sat on the empty stretcher opposite, and another one of the ski patrollers followed the ambulance in Bert's old Chevy.

"It was an accident," he said.

"He was a ski teacher," Sally said, realizing that neither the attendant nor the ski patroller had a clue to what she meant. He had done this deliberately, she was convinced. His last ploy to make her stay.

They took him into the emergency room of St. John's Hospital and she was told to stay in the waiting room. The doctors promised her that they would do everything possible and would tell her what his condition was as soon as they made their diagnosis. She waited, feeling the terrible agony of uncertainty, blaming herself for not heeding his pleas, fully comprehending that without her he had deemed his life worthless.

Her mind concocted terrible scenarios, a lifetime of paralysis and helplessness for him, and she promised herself that, if that was the case, she would remain at his side forever. I love you, my darling, she told him in her mind, feeling the terrible pain of emptiness and fear.

After an hour and a half of coping with the agony of suspense, one of the doctors came in, shaking his head.

"Are you his girlfriend?" he asked.

She nodded, unable to speak, watching his eyes, seeing no hints.

"I suppose you could say he's lucky," the doctor said.

"Lucky?"

"He's got three broken ribs, a cracked humorous." He gripped his own upper arm to illustrate where that was. "A broken ankle and a mild concussion."

"No spinal injury?" Sally asked, feeling slightly giddy with relief.

"None. He's going to be fine. Unfortunately, he'll be able to ski again." The doctor chuckled.

"Can I see him?"

"He's still groggy and we'll be putting him in a cast." The doctor looked at his watch. "Come back in about three hours. We'll transfer him to a hospital bed."

Three hours, Sally thought, remembering her early flight. Now she would have to go through all of that again, whether to stay or go. Only this time the circumstances were far more complicated.

She drove Bert's car back to their little apartment and, for a long time, sat in their one good upholstered chair and contemplated her life. The apartment was seedy and small with a double bed in a bedroom that was little more than a closet. There was a television set perched on a table made out of an old crate and three old bridge chairs and a bridge table with uneven legs that they used to eat on.

A portable old stereo lay on the floor in a corner of the room beside which were a pile of old, mostly Beatles tapes. The so-called kitchen was merely a counter with a two-burner stove and a small refrigerator. A couple of dented aluminum pots and a frying pan hung on the wall over the stove.

Without Bert's presence to light the place up, the apartment was a mess. She hadn't paid much attention to it before and, acknowledged to herself, probably could share the blame for its condition, although not its size or the mismatched broken-down furniture. The bed was simply a box spring on a mattress and, despite the fact that it was the scene of their frequent lovemaking, it looked grungy and unmade. The white sheets seemed yellow in the light from the single lamp that sat on a hanging shelf.

Our little love nest, she sighed, surveying the place, as if for the first time. Was this the way he had planned for them to live for the rest of their lives, the scene of their love's idyll? She went into the bathroom, which was lit by a single bare bulb. The toilet was leaking in a continual flush and the small sink was chipped, the basin stained with rust.

Love certainly was blinding and powerful. She hadn't paid any attention, none at all, to the condition of the apartment, and it startled her. Was this to be their future, a tiny substandard apartment with a clear view of the parking lot and the garbage cans? Rejecting money was one thing, rejecting even the most marginal creature comforts was quite another altogether.

In his arms and his aura and when they were confronted with the great beauty of the outdoors, it all sounded romantic and wonderful. But one had to go inside once in awhile to get out of the cold or the sun or the fury of the elements. Was this place to be their cozy little home, their fate?

Yes, their affair had been special and probably would not come around again in her lifetime, not with the same awesome intensity. Looking around her, she observed the evidence of its power. She hadn't even noticed her surroundings, the dirt, the depressing furnishings and fixtures.

After a couple of hours of arguing with herself, she decided that she had to perform the cruelest act of her life, to leave someone she loved when he needed her most. She packed her suitcase and wrote a note telling him how much she loved him, then she tore it up and realized that this was something she had to do in person.

It was nearing midnight when she arrived at the hospital. The receptionist told her that she could go in, and she went up to Bert's room. His ankle and his arm were in casts and there was a bandage round his head. But he was conscious. When she came into the room, he opened his eyes.

"What a dumb thing to do," Bert said. His voice sounded hoarse and weak.

"It was an accident," she said, bending down and kissing him on the lips.

"God, I'm going to miss your smell."

She was startled by his easy acceptance of her departure. She had been expecting more pressure to stay, especially now.

"And I'll miss yours."

He was quiet for a time as he looked at her, just staring and smiling, and she knew that he was etching her face into his mind.

"You've got to admit, Sally. I tried everything."

"It nearly killed you."

"Well, it should give me something to do when you're gone, concentrating on getting better." He chuckled. "Aren't I a damned stupid romantic idiot?"

"Yes, you are."

After a few moments of silence, Bert spoke. "You go on back to the apartment and get some rest before you catch your plane."

She nodded, tears filling her eyes.

"I'll love you always, Bert," she said, wondering if that was the whole truth, hoping it was.

"Go find your future babe," he whispered, then closed his eyes. She bent over and kissed the closed lids, then left the room.

Outside, she bundled into her coat. The temperature had dropped even more. She could tell by the feel of her icy tears.

# 7
# THE HORSE THAT
# KILLED PAT JENSEN

 The horse that killed Pat Jensen quietly munched the grass in the fenced pasture adjacent to the Jensen ranch house. Bob could see him from the big picture window of the living room, as well as from the window of the master bedroom he once had shared with Pat. He could see him when he walked from the front door to the garage or when he sat on the mower to cut the grass or walked to the repair sheds or the tack room.

There was no escaping him, both in reality and in his imagination. The image and the pervasive ubiquitousness of this horse never left his consciousness even when he slept. To him, it was an evil presence and it permeated his life.

Pat had named the horse Big Jim, a four-year-old strawberry roan, sixteen hands high, a bit tall for a quarter horse. She had owned him since he was a colt and had ridden him countless times, joining the cowboys pushing cattle, inspecting the stock, and riding the fences. She also had ridden him on the mountain and valley trails for recreation.

Pat had lavished tough love and affection on Big Jim and always carried carrots and sugar in her pocket to bribe, appease or show spontaneous affection for him. She would talk to him often, snout to snout, rub his brow affectionately and pat his long tapering neck. She would allow no one on the ranch to groom him but her. Everyone knew that Big Jim was Pat's favorite. She loved that horse and, it could be said, Big Jim loved her.

Big Jim had not been an easy horse to train. He had been downright ornery, but with skill and patience Pat had gotten him into shape. Not that there weren't occasional lapses, but Pat's method of employing "tough-love" tactics quickly brought Big Jim back into obedience.

Bob Jensen and Pat Friday had been married for two years when Pat had been killed. When they fell in love, Bob believed that he had been searching for her all of his life. They had both considered it a miracle to have found each other when both were in their mid-fifties. Each had been married once before. Pat had been widowed and Bob had been divorced, and they each had two children, now grown, who were starting families of their own.

They had met at the National Museum of Wildlife Art after a lecture about the grizzly during one of the Bob's vacation visits to Jackson Hole. Bob was a hunter, had shot big game in Africa and elk, bear and antelope in the United States and Canada. Wildlife was, therefore, a particular interest of his. They had hit it off immediately. By the end of a week they were madly in love with each other, and through their courtship and marriage, that fire had not dimmed.

Bob gave up his lucrative business career in Denver to join Pat at her ranch in Jackson Hole. Pat's parents, who were still alive and active, owned the adjacent ranch to Pat's and, although raising cattle was a losing proposition it was, for them, a way of life. Whenever cash flow was shrinking, they would sell off pieces of the large ranches to moneyed people moving out of the big cities in search of the healthy outdoor life.

Pat knew the day of ranching in this part of Wyoming was on the way out. The land was becoming too valuable not to develop, especially since only three percent of all the land in the valley was held in private ownership. But neither Pat nor her parents knew any other way to live. Raising cattle was their life's work. Bob understood this and a good part of his and Pat's relationship was built on the premise that ranching was the way they both would live out the rest of their lives.

The Fridays were a close and loving family, and Pat's children, Carl, a lawyer in Jackson, and Cindy, who ran a boutique selling Western clothes, both lived with their spouses in town. Pat's parents were the children of homesteaders who had come to the valley around the turn of the century and established the original ranches. Bob's children lived on the West Coast, but visited often.

As a married couple, Bob and Pat had never been happier in their lives. They were inseparable, eschewing Jackson's many social events to spend most of their time with each other. Bob helped Pat with the ranching chores. In summer, they rode the range and trails, floated down the Snake River fly-fishing for trout, and hiked or rode on the many valley and mountain trails. On weekends, they would have Pat's parents and children over for barbecue.

In winter, they would ski Rendezvous Mountain or cross-country on the ranch or in the national park. When they felt restless or a bout of cabin fever coming on, they would hop down to the Bahamas for bone fishing and scuba diving.

Life for Bob and Pat was an extended honeymoon. They were healthy and youthful and greedy for each other's company. They felt and acted like young lovers, as if discovering the joys of romance and sex for the first time. People remarked about how happy and loving they were.

Pat had grown up with horses. She had been riding since she was five years old and knew every facet of horsemanship. She could ride her horse along the narrowest ridges and switchbacks and over fences and streams. She knew how to ride so as to coax cattle to move slowly to reduce weight loss. She also knew the signs of ill health in horses and would inspect their legs, hooves, eyes and mouth for any signs of infection or injury.

Although Bob enjoyed riding and generally liked horses, he did not have much faith in the animal's intelligence. Pat, on the other hand, believed that a horse had what she called an "equine brain" that possessed a different intelligence which could render them passive aggressive, stubborn or clever and manipulative.

"Their instincts are for freedom," she told Bob often. "We've enslaved them to do our bidding. They would much rather run wild. Never blame the horse. Blame their human keepers."

Bob would never argue the point with Pat. He was a novice in terms of horsemanship and he respected Pat's opinion on most issues concerning cows, bulls, horses and ranching, in general.

"Never dispute the best cowboy in Wyoming," he would tell her. It was his most repetitive term of endearment.

"And you're the best dude in the valley," she would counter.

In retrospect, Bob had never been particularly fond of Big Jim. He couldn't put his finger on exactly why this was so. But he could not look Big Jim in the eye without feeling uncomfortable. When he told Pat of this feeling, she would laugh and declare that he was jealous.

"Any time and love lavished on man or beast that is not lavished on me provokes my jealousy," he would joke. There was some truth in that, he believed. But not the whole truth. Once he had tried to ride Big Jim, with near disastrous results. Inexplicably, Big Jim had bucked and thrown him sprawling into the dust.

"He's never done that," Pat told Bob. "Never."

"'Till now," Bob replied, rubbing his rear end, which had taken the brunt of his fall.

"I'll kiss away the hurt," Pat told him, laughing.

"Can I depend on that?"

"Word of honor," Pat said.

"In that case, I'll ride him daily," Bob said, reaching for Big Jim's pommel. But he never did ride Big Jim again.

His uncomfortable feelings about Big Jim did not go away. At times, the horse would lift his head and stare at him with, what Bob imagined, was threatening intent. He did not convey this feeling to Pat. Bob would feel this discomfort and antagonism even when they would ride together with the cattle or on recreational forays into the mountains.

Bob would note Big Jim's occasional look of malevolence when he gazed his way. You're being silly, he told himself, although, as a hunter, he had seen that look before, but it was always when he had a lethal weapon in his hands and could see the animal's expression in his sights.

Of course, he knew better than to superimpose human emotions and values on animals, especially horses. He often wondered whether or not they had "thoughts," or perhaps, mysterious inner processes that might be called emotion. He speculated that this might be true of dogs, but was not certain that the horse had evolved to that level of the canine.

In animal terms, Bob suspected that horses did possess a very rudimentary intelligence and a crude memory that was reinforced by repetition. In the case of Big Jim, Bob saw something quite different from ordinary animal intelligence. Big Jim's look of malevolence was palpable and, again in retrospect, unmistakable and clearly articulated. Big Jim, Bob had come to believe, despised him and resented his presence in Pat's life.

That day, he and Pat had not intended to work the cows. It was their second anniversary and they had planned to cuddle the day away in bed, drink champagne and have a private dinner at home.

The herd was scheduled to be brought from the pastures in the lower valley to those in the mountains. But a problem had arisen with the couple who were to lead the herd and move their goods to the cabin they shared during the cattle's stay in the mountain pastures, and Bob and Pat had to forego the pleasures of this special day to help push the cattle in the drive to higher ground.

As always, Pat rode Big Jim and Bob rode his favorite horse, "Scout," a gentle palomino with a good attitude and obedient ways. In riding up the high country, Big Jim showed no sign of skittishness. The day was bright and cloudless and both horses seemed fresh and eager.

"Good day for the drive," he remembered saying.

"The best."

"We'll get to the champagne later."

"For sure."

Pat rode point on Big Jim and Bob rode the flanks on Scout. A couple of cowboys took up the rear prodding strays. They moved with efficient progress with nothing unfavorable happening until Big Jim bucked suddenly, lifting his front legs high, clawing the air with his hooves. Pat calmed him skillfully, then got off the saddle, walked to the head of the horse, patted his neck and spoke to him snout to snout. The herd stopped moving.

"Hey buddy, what's wrong?" she asked the horse.

"Felt like bucking is all," Bob muttered.

"What do you suppose spooked him?"

"Ask the son-of-a-bitch."

"Don't call him that, Bob."

"All right, I won't call the bastard a son-of-a-bitch anymore," Bob replied with mock contrition. He looked toward the horse, catching the same malevolent look he seemed to have reserved for Bob.

"He doesn't mean that, Jim," Pat said to the horse. She took out a carrot from her pocket and gave it to him to munch.

"He doesn't deserve that," Bob growled, wondering if there was some jealousy in the remark.

"Pay no attention, Jim," Pat said to the horse. "You just concentrate on being a good boy. Hear?" She patted Big Jim's snout and watched him chew the last of the carrot.

"Sweet talk sure works," Bob said, chuckling.

Pat looked toward him and smiled.

"Works on most males," she said saucily.

"Even geldings?" Bob asked.

She shook her head and smiled.

"Stallions require a bit more effort," she said, winking, putting her foot on the left stirrup and swinging the other over Big Jim's haunches.

After a bit of restlessness, the herd began moving again. But Big Jim, despite his recent coddling, had his own ideas. He bucked again, but this time his buck was high and his clawed hooves threw him off balance. He had reared too high.

It all happened so fast Bob couldn't exactly fix it in his

memory. For some reason, Pat's right foot had slid off the stirrup and she had lost control of the horse. Instead of righting itself from the buck, Big Jim reared too far backward and all fours lifted from the ground.

The horse plummeted backward with Pat grasping the horn, reaching it, holding on. It was a futile gesture, dooming her by her attempt to balance herself and hold a firm seat on the saddle. The entire bulk of the horse, all 1,500-odd pounds of him, fell backward, directly on Pat, crushing her. The horse righted itself and quickly rose to a standing position, leaving Pat's crushed body on the high grass of the clearing.

It had all happened in seconds, but with enough power of retrieval to allow him to view it in his memory over and over again. He would see them both in slow motion, the horse and Pat, falling backward like dancers in a ballet, the horse falling on her like deadweight. No sound had come from either of them, no scream, no throaty cry of panic from the horse. All he had heard was the terrible thumping sound of a great weight hitting the ground and the baying of the cattle in the background.

Quickly, the two cowboys holding up the rear deflected the herd and pushed them out of the area where Pat had fallen.

Bob had dismounted quickly and kneeled beside his prostrate wife. She was still breathing, but the sound of it was labored and shallow and the pulse in her wrist was faint to his touch. He could see that the upper part of her body had caved in.

"Darling . . ." he began, then swallowed his words as he saw the life drain from her face. In the last flush of life she managed to raise an arm, but slightly, then point what seemed to Bob an accusing finger at the now standing and indifferent horse. In that gesture, he felt certain was no forgiveness, only the promise of vengeance. In the dying flicker of life in her eyes, he believed he saw her confusion, frustration, anger and regret. I loved you. Why have you done this to me? Had he heard these words mimed on her expiring lips?

For a brief moment, he was panicked. He had no idea what to do. He dared not lift her for fear of hurting her further. Then he remembered that she carried a cellular phone in her saddle bag. He ran to the now standing Big Jim, groped in her saddle bag and called for help.

As he spoke into the phone, he met Big Jim's gaze. Their eyes locked momentarily. The look of malevolence was still there, but he imagined that another message had superimposed itself in the horse's eyes, a smug message of victory and satisfaction. He was too concerned about Pat to contemplate the thought, running back to his wife, who now lay still as a rock. Putting his fingers on her wrist, he could not feel her pulse.

They were helicoptered to St. John's Hospital in Jackson, but the medic on the helicopter—after placing the head of his stethoscope on her caved chest—shook his head. She was dead.

It was, of course, the worst few days of his life. He had lost his true love, his best friend, his companion, his lover. The miracle between them had been abruptly terminated. Big Jim had destroyed the most important person in his world. Worse, he had dispatched her to a cold oblivion and robbed her of her life at the precise moment of her greatest happiness.

For days, he was inconsolable. He paced the rooms of the big house they had built. He felt disjointed, depressed and totally alone, like a walking dead man. Indeed, he contemplated taking his own life, joining Pat. Often he lifted his tear-stained face to the sky and imagined he was talking to his dear, dead wife.

"I ache for you, baby," he would call to her. "Come back to me." There was not even an echo of his own voice to reply.

His children came to visit, which helped somewhat. Pat's parents, both in their eighties, seemed to hold up much better than him.

"Proves you can't count on anything," Mrs. Friday told him through her tears. Mr. Friday was struck speechless with grief and did not say one word during the funeral or for days afterward. As it always is in close and loving families, the mourners banded together and provided each other with solace.

Then things calmed down and everyone went back to their lives. Bob's children went home and Pat's children began to pursue their various interests. As it had been agreed, the ranch would go to the children, but Bob would have the right to live in the house they had built until he died, if he so chose. It was not a question of money. Bob had ample funds. But without Pat, even wealth was meaningless. He had lost his only real treasure.

It was two weeks after the funeral that Big Jim caught Bob's attention again. The shock of Pat's death had blocked the horse and his deadly fall from his consciousness. The ranch wranglers had taken care of him, turning him out to the fenced meadows adjacent to the house. To Bob, he was both a menace and an eyesore and he tried his best to ignore him. His very presence became unbearable. Finally, he put it to Mr. Friday.

"He should be destroyed."

"He didn't do it on purpose," Mr. Friday argued. "Pat wouldn't have blamed him."

"He killed my wife," Bob said, tempted to bring up what

he had believed he observed in her dying moments. But he held his tongue.

"It was my daughter, Bob," Mr. Friday said.

"And my mother," Carl pointed out.

"But that horse has no right to live," Bob persisted.

"Mother loved that horse," Carl said. "You know that, Bob. You know how she felt."

"He murdered her," Bob muttered, swallowing the word "deliberately." Still, he did not bring up his impressions about Big Jim before Pat had been killed. They would have thought he had gone bonkers.

"Let's let it lie for awhile, Bob," Mr. Friday said.

Out of respect for Pat's memory, Bob did not want to offend the old man or Pat's son. There were other considerations as well. The horse belonged to Pat, not to him. Legally, it now belonged to Carl. At this moment in time, he realized, he was an outsider, his connection with the family tolerated, but, in fact, severed by Pat's death. With Pat gone, he had no role to play in her family matters.

After all, he had only come into Pat's life two years ago. She had already lived most of her life and had her own private baggage to carry. As did he. In the matter of the horse, he realized he had little to say about its disposition.

Following Mr. Friday's advice, he had let it lie. He had no idea about what future course he could chart for himself. He lived in the big house they had planned and built together, but his existence was empty and desolate. Without Pat, the house provided little comfort to him, other than a roof over his head.

Soon the house became a kind of prison or worse, a torture chamber. Wherever he went in the house or outside of it, he saw Big Jim. It was impossible to escape him and what Bob imagined was his smug look of satisfaction.

Often, the horse would lift its head when he sensed Bob's presence and turn to gaze at him. Bob would stare back, the bile of hatred churning in his chest. He would bring up the subject of Big Jim whenever he was with Mr. Friday or Carl.

From day to day, his hatred of Big Jim accelerated. He began to lose sleep over him, tossing and turning on his bed, aching for his lost wife and remembering her pointing at the horse as she died. What did she mean?

"Him," he imagined she had mimed. "I lim." Did it mean that she knew that Big Jim had deliberately killed her? The thought began to obsess him.

"You have got to get rid of that son-of-a-bitch," Bob told Carl one day.

By then, the horse and its role in his wife's death had become an obsession. Nothing he did could drive the idea from his mind. He had become convinced that the horse, by some mysterious inner logic, had decided that if he couldn't have Pat to himself he would eliminate her.

It wasn't exactly the kind of thought he could share with anyone. He had imposed a human mindset on an animal. It was impossible, his logical mind argued. Then the ultimate question would arise. Was it really?

At times, when he would look across the meadow at Big Jim, calmly munching his grass, he would be moved to a level of hatred he had never before experienced, and a stream of curses would roll loudly from his tongue. Disturbed by the sound, Big Jim would lift his neck and stare at him, taunting and haughty. Who is the real master here? his look seemed to imply.

"Look, Bob. Put Big Jim out of your mind. What's done is done," Carl replied.

"Does that mean you want to keep the horse?"

"Mom loved him."

"Well he didn't love her back."

Carl gazed at Bob and shook his head.

"Maybe you should get away for awhile Bob."

"Bet you'd like that, Carl. I'm sort of a third wheel here, anyway."

"You're too sensitive, Bob. We've all respected you a lot. Mom was happy with you."

"Your Mom is gone now." Bob felt a sob well up in his chest. "Yes, she was happy with me. It was the happiest time of her life. For me, too."

The sob rose in his chest and he turned away from Carl's gaze to mask it with a cough. In turning, he saw Big Jim again, watching them, the look of victorious smugness unmistakable. Between us, they want me to be the one to go, he thought.

"Maybe I will go somewhere for awhile," Bob said, turning again to face Carl. "Probably be a good thing to get away, go someplace that won't remind me of her."

"Great, Bob. Time heals. Hell, we're all hurt by this. We all loved her. She was my Mom. Cindy and I both miss her terribly."

Tears welled in his eyes and Bob knew his grief was heartfelt. Neither Carl nor Cindy had ever wanted to work the ranch, and Bob knew that when Pat's parents died they would be putting both ranches up for sale.

"I really think it would be best to get away, Bob," Carl said as a kind of final reminder before turning to walk back to his car.

"What about the horse?" Bob called to him, suddenly remembering that the subject of the conversation had been deflected.

Carl turned and gazed back at him.

"Mom wouldn't have wanted anything to happen to Big Jim," he said. "Leave it alone, Bob. Get away. It's over."

Then he turned and Bob watched him get into his car and drive out the ranch road, raising dust in his wake.

The next couple of weeks were agonizing for Bob. He roamed the big house like a lost soul. He no longer felt part of the ranch and, after some effort at helping with the ranch chores, he retreated from them. Besides, he was irrelevant to the operation of the ranch. The cowboys were taking orders from Carl now.

Without Pat around or the ranch chores to keep him busy, his focus became more and more centered on Big Jim. The horse seemed to have a favored position among the cowboys. No one would ride him, but he was always well groomed and given the run of the meadows.

His obsession with Big Jim grew and his hatred of the animal grew intense. It got so that he could not look at him without feeling a terrible sense of aggression. Occasionally, Pat's parents would invite him over for dinner and he would raise the question of the horse. If Carl was present, he would raise his eyes to the ceiling in obvious exasperation.

"Forget it, Bob," he would say, and the old people would nod their heads in agreement. Soon Bob gave up raising the question. The fact was that even the opportunity to bring it up was diminishing. They invited him less and less as time went on. Even the few friends that he and Pat socialized with when she was alive stopped calling, increasing his isolation.

But nothing could stop his thoughts about Big Jim. Imaginary conversations with the horse would pop into his mind at odd times. The horse would reply in body language, but the intent was always understandable.

"You murdered her, you monster."

Big Jim's head would rise and fall, clearly enunciating his reply.

"If I couldn't have her to myself, no one was going to," the horse seemed to reply.

"You robbed me of my life and happiness," Bob would say.

"You got that backwards, man," the horse seemed to reply. "It was you who robbed me."

"You deserve to die," Bob would say.

Again, the horse would motion with his big head, his mane rippling.

"You don't own me. You have nothing to say about it."

"I can't stand the sight of you," Bob would say.

"Then pack up and leave," the horse would reply in his body language.

No matter how hard Bob tried to get the horse out of his mind, he could not. Big Jim permeated his thoughts to the exclusion of all else. Finally, Bob knew it was time to leave or he would lose his mind.

He supposed the only place for him to go was to the West Coast where he would be able to see his children from time to time. He still owned half the house he and Pat had built and he told Carl either to buy out his half or give it to a real-estate firm to sell. He didn't care either way. Without his beloved Pat to share it with him, money was hardly relevant. He had more than enough to live on.

On the night before the final day of his departure, he bid goodbye to Pat's parents and children. Although he told them that he might come back, he knew that he would never see them again. Apparently, they had the same feeling and their goodbyes had a sense of finality about them.

He awoke before dawn and packed his remaining possessions in his car. The spires of the Tetons were just beginning to catch the orange glow of the rising sun and he watched them for a long moment, his mind and heart offering a final farewell. In their shadow, he had had his happiest moments and his deepest despair.

. Pulling the car out of the garage, he prepared to drive down the ranch road, but his attention was arrested by Big Jim. He was galloping along the fence parallel to the car. Suddenly he reared, his forelegs clawing the air as he had done when Pat was riding him. The gesture seemed to Bob the ultimate exhibition of victory, a final celebration of his antagonist's surrender.

The horse's taunt exploded in Bob's mind. He made a quick U-turn and proceeded back to the storage shed where ranching equipment was stored. The horse stood stock still for a few moments, then cantered to the edge of the fence near the shed.

Bob went into the shed and unhooked a large ax, then moved over the fence and stood, as Pat had often done, snout to snout, offering words of affection. He did not pat the horse's neck with his free hand. He had no desire to touch him with his flesh.

He looked into the horse's eyes. The malevolence still glowed inside of them, buttressing the rage ready to burst in Bob's gut. He moved back one step and swung the ax with all his strength, hitting the horse square on its head. He could hear the shattering bone as the cutting edge split the head apart.

He watched the fire go out of the horse's eyes as the horse sank slowly to the ground as if in supplication. Again, he lifted the ax and, swinging it sideways this time, cut a huge swath in the horses' neck. The horse fell on its side. His breath coming in short gasps, Bob struck again and again until the horse's head was completely severed.

Still, his rage was not appeased. He flung the bloody ax to the ground and dragged the head by the mane to a fence post then lifted it and placed it on the post. For a long moment, he watched the glazed dead eyes, as if waiting for some silent comment in their expression.

When none came, he felt the rage empty from his body, like water from a broken dam. He looked up at the clear blue morning sky.

"All along, it was him or me," he thought. This was their destiny.

He knew they could never understand. The horse, after all, was the symbol of the West, a free spirit tamed by man to do his bidding. He was revered, worshipped, loved.

They would think of him as a destroyer, a killer, a man who had acted against nature. Who could ever blame the horse?

Nor did he blame all horses, only this one who had killed his love and wrecked his life. He felt no contrition, no remorse.

After awhile, he went back to his car, got in and drove out the ranch road, not looking back.

*8*

# *I LEFT MY SOUL HERE*

 The 737 tipped its wings for the wide turn that would point the plane due south and bring it in line with the runway landing from the north. From his vantage in the first-class cabin, Proctor could make out Blacktail Butte, Antelope Flats and Sheep Mountain, where one day in 1925, a third of it slipped off its natural mooring, bottled up the Gros Ventre river and formed a huge lake.

Odd how such landmarks had stuck in his mind, he thought, amazed at the recall that was flooding into his mind. As the plane moved lower and locked into its landing pattern at the small Jackson Hole airport, he could see the Teton Range, in all its craggy glory in the cloudless sky. Alongside the range, like a gray chalkmark written by an unsteady hand, meandered the Snake River, making its relentless way southward through the valley.

He tamped down an involuntary sob, clearing his throat

to mask it from his seated neighbor, a fresh-faced female college student heading for a summer job at one of the valley dude ranches. She had reminded him of his daughters at an earlier age. Reluctantly, he had exchanged pleasantries. The exchange was brief. He had no wish to talk, his thoughts and concentration were elsewhere.

As they came lower, he could see the tops of the houses that dotted the sagebrush plain. None had been there in his day. This part of the valley had all been ranch country, and it surprised him to see that it was barren of cattle.

"How beautiful," the college student mumbled.

"Yes," he agreed, but to him it was more than picture postcard static beauty. It was his youth, breaking through the dikes of memory, the half-century of self-imposed exile and denial. It was as if a long-closed dustless vault had opened, revealing the old images in mint condition, pristine. He was coming home, and his heart was full of wonder and regret.

Jackson Hole was only four hours from Calgary by jet— but eons away if one used a different concept of dimension, his mind's special measure. It was incredible to think that for years he had been only four hours away.

He could not recall exactly how long it had taken him to make the original hegira from Jackson Hole to Calgary. That had been a journey of escape, a run for his life. Recalling it now, it seemed merely a moment, like Alice taking a single step through the looking glass to another world. With that action, he had been reborn.

To do this, he had deliberately excised his first eighteen years from the recorded history of his life. He had recreated himself. He had been Robert Henry Proctor for fifty years, with a forged and fictional early history known only to himself. Of course, repetition had made it truth in the minds of his wife, his children, his friends, his bankers, his business associates, his immediate world. At times, he had even believed it himself. Such is the power of denial.

Thankfully, his reincarnation had come before the computer and now his creation, his resculpted self, was locked forever in electronic memory, the modern reality. The boy from Jackson Hole had disappeared.

He was now, literally, Robert Henry Proctor, Toronto, son of Mary and James Proctor, she a schoolteacher, he a free lance writer. Born December 15, 1928, Rector's Hospital, Toronto. Actually, the date was his true birth date, the only authentic documentation in his dossier.

Stealth and fraud and the blind luck of meeting people who could do that sort of thing had made him a true Canadian. Later, he had joined the Royal Canadian Army and become documented further, fingerprinted and otherwise identified. For more than half a century, he had been the real thing, certified and validated in the reality of data banks. The first eighteen years of his life no longer existed, except in his mind.

He had been goaded into the resurrection of this earlier period of himself by fear. The fear had arrived at his doorstep simultaneously with his quadruple bypass. He was certain that it had entered his psyche during anesthesia, seeped into his drugged dream and parked itself irrevocably in his brain.

Although he had temporarily beaten back death, he could not beat back the necessity of his resurrection. Exile had only emphasized the persistence of his identity. He had wandered in the desert ten years longer than Moses and his people and now he was coming home to the promised land of his soul. Since the epiphany he experienced, he supposed, in his drugged dream, he had come to believe such a thing implicitly.

The plane landed smoothly, and although he could have been one of the first to exit, he had remained in his seat, unable to find the courage to move. Finally, the desire to set foot on the treasured land of his heart won out and he rose, took his small duffel and exited.

The June air was crisp and slightly dizzying. It was, he knew, more than just the altitude. He was stunned by the familiarity, the overwhelming shock of recognition and the joy of return. His heart pounded and he stopped for a moment to catch his breath.

Turning, he saw the Grand Teton, still capped with a snowy hat, which would shrink in summer but still remain. A sudden spasm of tears dimmed the image and he turned away from it and moved on.

The airport seemed immense compared to what it had been in his day, but it was still small and a far cry from airports he had experienced elsewhere. He arranged for a rented car and was soon heading out to the highway, riding toward town.

He did not have any fixed destination, only that he was going to roam around and explore the various landmarks of his youth. He suspected that this was not his primary agenda, which remained deliberately vague in his mind. What he was certain of was that he needed this return, that his life would never be complete without this closing of the circle.

Perhaps this closing would consist simply of observing, penetrating what modernity and progress had done to his splendid valley and recounting in memory how it once had been. He was not sure how long he would stay and had not made any reservations as if to do so might commit him to a time-frame he was not prepared to fill.

Perhaps through the cruel coating of age he would recognize someone he had gone to school with, a buddy.

Maybe even Clara, his long-lost love. Maybe he would spend time here reminiscing with her or any person who had been around when he was growing up. Or maybe he would simply meander aimlessly, observe those landmarks of past memories and turn tail back to the airport and to Calgary.

This ambivalence was troubling. Was it merely compulsion that had brought him here? Or was there a sense of mission? Having arrived, he still was not certain. Clara, if she were alive, would be his age. Only one feature stood out in his memory, her eyes, as blue as the winter sky, large and deep. Once he had thought that looking into her eyes revealed the whole story of her inner life, the absolute truth of herself. Perhaps things had gone awry when he discovered the falsity of this assumption.

Beyond the memory of those eyes, he could barely recall any other of her physical characteristics, although, for years after he had gone, fleeting but vague images of her in those last days would float in and out of memory. Time had dimmed them and continued denial had almost extinguished them.

But recall had, since his bout of fear, opened the vault of earlier memories. Clara and he had been childhood playmates, then schoolmates. His parents had died in a car crash when he was ten years old and he was raised by his Aunt Agatha, who lived in a modest house in town. A childless widow, she was a pinched and frugal woman who, although respecting her obligations to her orphaned nephew, did not have the capacity to give anything more than material comfort to the boy she was raising.

Despite this, he could now clearly remember the life of small town Jackson Hole in those days. It was a child's paradise, filled with wondrous outdoor activities. As a young boy, his father had taught him to ride horses, fly fish, downhill ski and hunt. He had tried to replicate this loving instruction with his own children, fictionalizing his early days as if they had occurred on Canadian soil. Yet, he had never truly felt that he had quite recaptured the elegance and feeling of his father's instruction. There was always something missing, a dead spot that could not be felt or glimpsed.

He had never expected to leave Jackson Hole. While others among his schoolmates might have yearned for a more materially successful life out in the bigger world, he had been content to project his future in Jackson, making his living in whatever capacity came along. He had no ambitions beyond the valley. Nor did Clara.

What had bedeviled him most about his recall of the old memories had been the fact that he could be so consumed by passion and jealousy as to drive him to commit an act so opposed to any of his perceived natural tendencies before or since. He must have loved Clara with a passion so overwhelming as to defeat all reason. He must have been a man possessed, a man so consumed by desire as to render him irrational and, as it turned out, murderous.

Nor could he find in his memory any replication of that emotion. It was as if it had happened to someone else, perhaps his obliterated younger self. Never in the subsequent years of his life had he felt anything so deeply.

He and Clara had become lovers at sixteen and it was a given in the mind of his Aunt and Clara's parents that after high school they would be married and raise a family in the valley. All this was a foregone conclusion until the appearance of Ezra Farmer, a cowhand at the Barber ranch, a drifter who had, as most cowboys in those days, simply appeared.

The Barber ranch was north of town, adjacent to the ranch of Clara's parents. By the standard of the times, neither family was considered well-off. Ranching in the Jackson Hole climate was a tough and grubby job, more a way of life than a road to fortune.

Henry Proctor, who was not Henry Proctor then but Mason Jansen, could not recall how Ezra and Clara had met. It was probably more an accident of proximity than anything else. They simply appeared together. It seemed, at first, a friendly and purely platonic relationship. Ezra was a narrow-hipped, craggy-faced, easygoing, laid-back, drawling cowboy type about two years older than them.

Nor could Mason remember what had triggered his suspicions, only that it had inspired surveillance on his part. He had, he recalled, confronted Clara on the subject.

"He's just a friend," Clara had protested.

"He seems more than a friend," Mason had countered.

"You're being silly and jealous."

"Am I really?"

"Yes."

He had looked into her eyes. Did he see the truth in them or was it an illusion?

After awhile, if memory served, he had desisted from confrontation. But his suspicions persisted and soon he was spending nights camped not far from the repair cabin on the Barber ranch where Ezra had his bunk. He could not even remember his animosity, only that he was watchful and suspicious. His jealousy must have reached a kind of fevered pitch and his imagination surely had run rampant.

As he might have expected, his surveillance bore fruit. He saw Clara come out of the repair shop after midnight. It was September, he remembered, as the hunting season had begun. His reaction had to be devastating, although he could not, after all those years, summon up the true corrosive reaction of jealousy. He concluded that it must have made him crazy, his manhood challenged, leaving him thirsting for revenge.

Apparently he had not confronted Clara with the evidence of his observations. It was a simple case of unfaithfulness, a condition that hardly entered his consciousness in his relationship with his wife of more than forty-five years. It was unthinkable.

Was it because he could never summon up the passion that he once had felt for Clara? He had, he supposed, felt something for his wife at the time of his courtship and marriage. She had never triggered a jealous eruption. In fact, he had come to realize that his true emotional life was bland and secretly indifferent. He had been dutiful but not passionate. He behaved as a loving husband and father, but he questioned his own sincerity and it troubled him. Compared to what he had experienced with Clara, life with his wife was pallid and bland.

He had been warned that a heart bypass operation could have emotional consequences, perhaps even trigger depression. What he knew he felt was a vague sense of longing. This sense had grown until he realized that what he had longed for was his past, his place, his roots, his old feelings of attachment and belonging.

He could barely remember the events leading up to the incident that had changed his life. Had it been planned? Could he possibly have conceived such an idea? Yet he could remember the hurt and humiliation engendered by Clara's perceived betrayal.

The hunt must have been his idea. He had always hunted elk in late September. It had been a way of life. As a small boy, he had hunted with his father and could remember watching him field dress the animal and take it back to the house tied to his truck, providing the family with a winter's worth of stew.

He, Mason, had his father's hunting rifle, he remembered, while Ezra had to borrow a rifle from the Barbers. They drove into the Teton wilderness in his beat-up old Ford pickup, also a legacy from his father. He could recall the long walk up from the trailhead in search of elk still foraging in the high country before their remarkable trek, after the first snows, to the National Elk Refuge in Jackson.

Mason was not certain whether the hunting trip had been arranged before he had discovered Clara coming out of Ezra's quarters or after. He could acknowledge, even in memory, that he must have harbored murderous thoughts about Ezra, although he could not recall any plan to actually make such thoughts reality.

That day, the weather was overcast with sporadic rain clouds coasting through the valley. Up high, the snows had begun their relentless trek from the high peaks downward. Native hunters like himself were an intrepid lot and were not deterred by inclement weather, unless it made stalking impossible.

They moved up into the high country, already ankle deep in snow. Had Mason confronted Ezra about Clara? He couldn't remember or he had blocked it out. They must have spotted elk. He could recall shots being fired, but no kills. They started down a path that ran beside one of the canyons. It began to snow, the flakes thick and relentless. Looking south toward the draw—the usual route of the weather—Mason could see clear sky. There seemed no cause for alarm.

Unfortunately, the snow grew more intense and Mason could barely see in front of him. Ezra walked ahead of him. He had a vague recollection of lifting his rifle, taking aim at the back of Ezra's head, hearing the shot, feeling the kick. What was etched in his mind was his own anger and his humiliation, his murderous thoughts, his sense that Ezra had stolen Clara's love.

What he did remember clearly was that Ezra had simply disappeared from view and Mason had run to where he had last seen him. He could see footprints and an indentation on the white snow where Ezra must have slid into the canyon. From his vantage, he could not see Ezra's body. He remembered calling out his name, hearing the echo coming back. He had, he was certain, attempted to find another path to the bottom of the canyon, but it eluded him. The snow was relentless and eventually he had to give up the search.

He had no trouble recalling his panic and confusion. Worse, he remembered that he had actually felt elation, and this troubled him. He would never be certain how he had conceived the idea in his own mind, but he had declared himself instantly guilty.

He had fantasized such a fate for Ezra and it had occurred. People were sure to believe he was guilty of murder. An investigation would have left him vulnerable. They would easily discover that he was the deceived lover tempted to vengeance.

Whatever the logic of his thinking at that moment, he made his decision. He fled. He did not look back. He made his way down to the trailhead, got into his pickup, headed north and did not stop until he had crossed the Canadian border. He remembered, too, that he had thrown his rifle over the railing of a high bridge somewhere, the location long forgotten.

From that moment to this, he had not set foot in Jackson Hole. He made no inquiries. He had no knowledge of any aftermath of this event. He never contacted his Aunt Agatha or Clara again or, for that matter, any of the people he had known during his first eighteen years of life.

He had panicked into flight and self-imposed exile. Whatever the true circumstances of this act, he had proclaimed himself guilty. He could never face Clara again. To be torn from his roots, from his beloved valley, seemed at the time rough justice and he was certain that he deserved this punishment.

After a year or two, he ceased to speculate what Clara might have thought of him and, as time passed, he erased such speculations from his mind. As for his Aunt Agatha, he believed that his departure had been more of a relief than a concern and he had never dwelled on it.

Then had come the operation and its aftermath. His thoughts about his life in Jackson Hole became obsessive. He was assailed by memory, which preoccupied his every waking hour and seeped into his dreams. His return was far from a whim. It was a necessity.

Nobody in the world knew he was here, not even his wife, Barbara. Certainly not any of his four children, grown now and living scattered throughout Canada and the States. He had informed Barbara that this was a business trip, although he rarely traveled for business anymore. His son, Bob, ran the real-estate agency, the largest in the province. His own designation now was "consultant", which meant that he kept up his old friendships and contacts for the benefit of the business.

The real-estate agency had been good to them. He was a rich man, a far cry from the frightened impoverished string bean of a boy who had arrived in Calgary fifty years before. He could not be certain whether or not Barbara believed his story about responding to a call from an old client in

Halifax who was mulling a deal in Calgary, but that was less his concern than his own necessary objective. He would call her tonight and pretend he was calling from Halifax. There was no sense dragging her into it at this late date.

He drove the rented car toward town. He had expected change, and there were still enough recognized sights to satisfy his sense of home. The Elk Refuge hadn't changed at all. In three months, it would be filled with thousands of winter occupants. He could see the town ski area, wide brown swaths crawling up Snow King mountain waiting for the snow to arrive.

The town square remained as he remembered it, a tree-studded patch of green with four entrance gates, one at each corner, each topped with elk antlers. The stores surrounding the square had changed, but the wooden sidewalks were still intact and he could recognize the outlines of some of the buildings, gussied up now to attract trade.

He drove his car slowly east of the square, past what once was his parent's house, which, miraculously had remained recognizable, although he was too overwhelmed with emotion to linger long. He could not find his Aunt Agatha's old house and assumed that it either had been remodeled beyond recognition or had been demolished.

In his mind, he could eliminate the growth that had occurred in the fifty years since he had been here last. The mountains and the landscape that had been part of his early life remained untouched. These natural wonders triggered memories, arousing in him the satisfying sensation of truly returning home.

For the first time since he had touched the land of his birth, he had a firmer grasp of why he had come. He realized that he wanted more than simply closure. He wanted a kind of confirmation that he had been born and lived in this place. He wanted the return of his eighteen lost years. He needed proof positive that he once had walked these streets, had looked out upon these mountain ranges, had breathed the sweet clean crisp air.

Parking his car, he went into the drugstore at the northwest corner of the square, which actually had been there in his day, although it had been modernized beyond recognition. None of the faces were familiar to him, yet he did not feel like a stranger. At the counter, he bought one of the local newspapers and noted that behind the clerk was a telephone and beside it a directory.

"May I borrow that?" he asked the clerk, pointing to the directory. The clerk nodded her consent and handed him the book. In his day, the telephone directory was a thin affair and all numbers were in four digits. Compared to Calgary, though, it was still thin and, putting on his half glasses, he thumbed through the pages looking for familiar names.

Since Aunt Agatha had been his only relative, his last name had little relevance, although he did discover a list of Harpers, which was Clara's family name, a fairly common name in the valley. But there were none named Clara. He did recognize some names that might have been from his time, but he had no intention of calling them or declaring himself.

It was highly probable that the reason for his flight years ago had long been forgotten, but he did fear that there might still be people living who would remember. There was no point in risking recognition. After all, there was no statute of limitations on the crime of murder, although he speculated that, at this late stage, acknowledgment would be more a media event than a risk of incarceration. If word did get out, his family would be appalled at the revelation. After all, he had lived a lie. He left the drugstore and went back to his car.

Turning west, he drove into more unfamiliar territory, although the buttes and mountain backgrounds remained as recognizable landmarks. A number of shopping centers and automobile dealerships had sprung up along the highway route, which once had been a narrow road sparsely traveled.

Driving south toward Hoback Junction, he turned right at what he remembered was the old Melody Ranch and headed toward the old cemetery where his parents were buried. It amazed him how quickly he found his direction after all those years. The old cemetery road quickly became familiar.

It would be going on sixty years since he had attended the funeral of his parents and it astounded him how powerfully the old grief had grabbed him. He felt a brief moment of hysteria as he parked the car and headed toward the iron gate that enclosed the cemetery. There was, of course, a lot more headstones than had been there at the time of his parents' burial.

For a time, he stood by the gate, trying to remember exactly where his parents had been buried. Looking up, he saw the Teton Range and remembered what he had seen when he looked up to hear the minister's prayer as both of his parents were lowered into the ground. Moving into the cemetery, he passed headstones of familiar names.

He recognized those of his old schoolteachers, the minister who had buried his parents and whose church he had attended, names of old ranching families and even some of his own contemporaries who had been his school chums. There were Simpsons and Hansens and Woods and Barbers and Lucases and Wilsons, old families of his time, which he recognized.

Finally, he found the simple headstone on which his

parents names had been carved. Apparently, the cemetery was well cared for and there was evidence that weeds around the headstone had been pulled recently.

"Died 1938," the headstone read, "Molly and Brett Jansen, beloved father of Mason," then the dates of his parents' birth and death. His mother hadn't been thirty yet and his father had been thirty two. Mason had lived more than twice as long as either of them. Tears filled his eyes as he looked down upon the grave.

"Mama. Papa," he heard himself say as a shudder ran through him. How was it possible that he had not paid homage to them in their burial ground in more than half a century? The guilt of that crime of disrespect assailed him, but he did feel again the power of a child's love of his parents for which he was grateful. He was feeling again, he told himself, and that was an occasion for rejoicing.

To the right of his parents' headstone was one commemorating Aunt Agatha, who was recorded as dying two years after he had left town. She was his father's spinster sister and had done her best to raise him. Despite her inability to show affection, she had been a good person and he had treated her shabbily. Just one more thing to add to his list of regrets, he thought, suddenly dissolving again in tears.

He stopped his crying and took a few deep breaths. Then his eye caught an adjacent headstone on the left of that of his parents. He looked at it in stunned silence, unbelieving.

"Mason Jansen, born December 28, 1928, Died September 26, 1946. RIP."

He couldn't believe his eyes. Suddenly he felt his heart pounding erratically. Then his knees buckled and he felt dizzy and on the verge of fainting. Recovering somewhat, he found himself kneeling at the site of his own grave. The utter irony of the situation, once the shock had subsided, goaded him into a wry chuckle. How would he respond if someone suddenly arrived and asked the question: Did you know him well?

Making no effort to stand up, he knelt before the headstone for a long time, trying to make sense of the situation. For a brief moment, his thoughts flirted with the supernatural. Perhaps the body below had been his and by some weird ghostly process his spirit had entered this other body, the body of Henry Proctor. Looking around him, he saw the Teton Range and the gently undulating landscape between the buttes, which recalled him to his sense of place and he rejected the supernatural.

Finally, he managed to stand up and brush off the knees of his pants. He still felt slightly shaky, but the pounding in his chest had receded. Rationality had returned and he reasoned that a body had been found, which had been mistakenly identified as his own. It did not take him long to take the leap of faith that under the headstone that bore his name was the corpse of Ezra Farmer. It gave him no comfort to know that his identity had already been obliterated by the time he began his own process of eliminating his past.

But the revelation served to give him a sense of mission. He had found a more concrete reason for his return. Getting into his car, he drove to where he remembered the public library had been. It was still located in the same log building on King Street and had changed little, although a sign announced that a new library was being built.

Inside, he poured over the telephone directory and copied out names that he had remembered from his youth. Then he got a handful of quarters from the librarian and, posting himself at the pay phone at the foot of the stairs, he began to make calls.

Jackson, after all, was still a small town, despite the

passage of years. It had always been an open friendly place and he found this still to be true. People went out of their way to be helpful.

"I'm just passing through and looking for an old friend," he told those who answered. He did not have to make too many calls to discover Clara Harper's history. She had married Tom Kelly, another schoolmate who he remembered vaguely. Tom had died about fifteen years ago and she had married Sam Parker, who also had died. Two children from her first marriage were living out of the valley and, yes, Clara had built a house on what was left of the old family property north of town.

"What did you say your name was?" the last person he had spoken to, asked. It was a man and, he was judging from his voice, an old-timer.

"Proctor," he said. "Henry Proctor."

"You say you're from here?"

"A long time ago," he had acknowledged.

"Can't say I remember any Proctors."

"Guess we didn't make much of a stir," Mason told the man, noting that he had adopted the old speech rhythms of valley people of his era.

It was late afternoon when he got to what he assumed was the old ranch road to the Harper place, now properly asphalted. The old-timer had given him careful directions. Along the way, he had noted that the Barber ranch had literally disappeared. The old main house and various outbuildings, including the one outside of which he had waited to discover Clara's infidelity, were gone. The ranch obviously had been subdivided and there were a number of large log homes where cattle once had grazed.

He had deliberately not called ahead, fearing that Clara might be too shocked by his sudden return to life and think he was some kind of a charlatan up to no good. Other than the road itself, nothing was as he remembered it. Like the Barber ranch, the Harper ranch had been subdivided and given over to large homes, which now dotted the landscape.

He followed the road until it ended and another road of dirt and gravel led through the trees almost to the river. A wooden sign proclaimed that this was the Parker place. A late model Ford Explorer stood in the winding driveway of a modest log house.

With great trepidation and hoping he would not shock the person who answered the door, he pounded the knocker. The door swung open. A wiry gray-haired woman stood in front of him and seemed to study his face. There was no mistaking who she was. He could tell by the eyes, their blue still as piercing and alert as they had been in her youth.

"I'll be damned," Clara said, opening the door wider in a gesture for him to be admitted. They continued to stare at each other as he came into the house. It confused and surprised him that she was not shocked by his presence.

"I'm Mason," he said, his voice choking.

"No kidding," she said, smiling. He noted that she had aged well and although she was grandmotherly and paunchy, her skin was hardly lined. Oddly, her voice seemed youthful, the way he remembered it. His assessment of himself was about the same. He believed he looked a few years younger than his age, but not much. They would both be taken for people in their mid-sixties, although they were merely a year from entering their seventh decade.

"I was expecting you for some time, Mason," Clara said, leading him to the living room, comfortably furnished in Western style. The ceiling was vaulted, with a large picture window that looked directly up at the Grand.

"Somebody tell you I was looking for you?" Mason asked.

She shook her head.

"I just knew you'd be back someday," she said. "Can I get you a drink or something?"

He declined but continued to study her. She had shown surprise by his sudden appearance but no shock.

"How could you know?" he said.

"I just knew," she shrugged.

Despite the distance of more than fifty years, he sensed a familiarity and it stirred in him an old warmth and affection. It was hardly the passion she had inspired years ago, although he could not deny the old feeling of sharing a deep secret. In those earlier years, their lovemaking was considered outside the moral code of the times.

His mind crowded with things to say that he could not express. His surprise at her reaction had stunned him. Indeed, everything that had happened since his return had been a surprise. For a long time, they were both silent as they observed each other. Finally he spoke.

"I've been to the cemetery," he said, his voice choking.

"I figured you would."

"Quite a shock to discover that I've been dead for more than fifty years," he said, trying to put a spin of humor on the circumstances. The afternoon sun was slanting into the room, throwing a pleasant orange glow everywhere. It had a happy feel, hardly gloomy at all.

"And here you are, alive and, I must say, looking pretty good," Clara said. "I'd say you must have had a good life, Mason."

"I guess I can't complain," he said lightly. She had put him at ease. Seeing her in this atmosphere had dispelled his earlier sense of shock.

"I know you're wondering about that business at the cemetery," she said. She sat down on the couch and insisted he

sit down on the leather easy chair. He obeyed, noting that
the chair swiveled.

"Joe loved that chair," she said. "Poor Joe. Gone two years
now." Her eyes moistened for a moment, then cleared. "I've
buried two." She chuckled. "Three. If you count yourself."

"Just one spouse for me, Clara. I've got three children
and five grandchildren." He was tempted to show her pictures, but resisted, although he wasn't sure why.

"I've got two kids and two grandchildren," Clara said.
"They both left the valley. Tough to make a living here,
Mason. If it wasn't for the land my parents left, I'd probably
be struggling myself. Both my husbands left very little."

"I've been pretty lucky, Clara. Money is not a worry."

Suddenly, the idea of money seemed irrelevant. They
were silent for a long time.

"So here we are, Mason, a couple of survivors."

"Not according to that stone in the cemetery."

He wanted to tell her about his life, his change of name
and identity, but he held back.

"Your Aunt Agatha and I identified the body," Clara said,
after another long silence between them.

"But surely . . ." He began. She lifted her hands palms
outward.

"We knew it wasn't you, Mason. But it wasn't until spring
that the body was found and by then . . . well, the animals
and elements had done their work. There was hardly anything left." She shook her head. "It wasn't a very pretty sight."

"My God," Mason said.

"Too many years have passed to remember how guilty I
must have felt. I did feel awful, Mason. I mean . . . well
what I did with Ezra obviously set you going. I had no idea
how it would affect you. I was so young." Her voice trailed
off and her blue eyes seemed to glaze over.

"So was I. Young and stupid."

"Things like that meant so much then."

"I barely remember how I felt, Clara. And that's the truth."

"Poor Ezra," Clara sighed. "He was such an innocent. Just a sad drifter. Actually, I felt sorry for him." She looked up suddenly and seemed to shiver. "I've always believed it was all my fault."

"It's done and gone, Clara," Mason said.

"Actually, I haven't really thought about it much."

"Neither have I."

"It was hard to believe, Mason," Clara said. "It was so out of character. You were not a violent person."

"No, I never was."

"I felt I owed you this, Mason. It was me that made you crazy with jealousy. I didn't have a clue. I liked Ezra. But I loved you, Mason. It's still vivid in my mind. Not the feeling itself. But the idea that I did love you."

He was trying to recall what that had meant.

"Nothing since showed me how much I mattered to someone. That someone was you, Mason. I've gone through two husbands, and I know they loved me. But I don't think I ever mattered as much to them as I did to you."

"Yes," he said, searching inside of himself for any remains of that old feeling, finding none. Nor had he ever found it with Barbara.

"I was surprised your Aunt Agatha went along. I told her everything. She was always such a straight arrow. I think maybe she was embarrassed and wanted the whole thing forgotten."

He wasn't quite sure he was following her, but he listened politely, his comments merely acknowledgments.

"We both knew you had fled. That was pretty obvious. Also that the chances were you wouldn't be coming home, not soon anyway." At that, she smiled. "Who would have figured fifty years?"

"Proves we only get one shot at life," Mason said. It occurred to him suddenly that he was studying this stranger, an older woman, her face and body misshapen by age. He was certain she had reached the same conclusion. He stood up and moved toward the window, looking out, his eyes searching what was beyond the glass, the river, the mountains, the trees, his valley. His eyes filled with tears. She must have seen. He felt her hand touch his shoulder gently.

"They don't get old like us, Mason," she whispered. "We come and go and they go on forever."

"I belonged here. I left my soul here," he managed to say. She handed him a tissue and he wiped his eyes and nose. Then he looked at her again, concentrating on her eyes, the look he had remembered so vividly. She moved into his arms and they embraced for a long time. "But I was afraid and I was guilty."

She insinuated herself out of his arms and studied his face.

"Then you did push him into the canyon. We assumed that, but we were never certain."

"Push?"

"What remained of his body was found at the bottom of the canyon. We just assumed. . . ."

"No," he said, concentrating on his memory. "I can't seem to remember that. It was one of those short-lived fall blizzards. I remember that. And the shot."

"Shot?"

"I believe I aimed at the back of his head and pulled the trigger."

She looked at him for a long moment. He felt as if her stare was penetrating him, looking inside his head.

"There was no sign of that, Mason. They said he died of a broken neck. From the fall. He wasn't shot."

"Wasn't. . . ."

Mason swallowed hard, struggling to find that tiny bit of recall. Had he missed or had he, at the last moment wavered in his aim. He had been a crack shot in those days and there was no way he would have missed at that distance. It occurred to him then that recall was impossible and the event would remain shrouded in denial and mystery, always tentative. Since that moment, he had never touched a firearm again.

"Perhaps the shot panicked him and he lost his balance," Mason said. "It would still make me guilty."

"Maybe," Clara said. "Or maybe not."

"And Ezra, what did they think happened to him? Considering that you and my Aunt told them that it was my body."

"Ezra had already given notice. He was set to move on anyway." She looked at him and shook her head. "Your death was ruled an accident."

The revelation left him confused and slightly disoriented. The passion of youth had confused his judgment and exiled him forever. It was a thought that triggered more regrets, and he quickly tamped it down. Long ago, he had mastered the art of denial. What he needed now was the courage to move on, leave the past behind.

"Sure there's nothing I can get you?" Clara asked.

He shook his head.

"Maybe it was better to leave the past buried," he sighed.

"When you think about it, Mason, it was only a small part of our lives."

"Timewise," Mason whispered. In his heart, he knew otherwise.

He embraced Clara again.

"I better get going," he said. "Plane to catch." He would drive back to the airport and get on the first plane to take him back to Salt Lake City and home to Calgary. He had better get back to being Henry Proctor before regrets overwhelmed him.

Clara accompanied him to the door, then turned again to face him.

"I never did, Mason. Not with Ezra. We talked is all. I liked him. But I was your girl. Tell you the truth, I've always been your girl."

They locked eyes for a long while. But by then he was Henry Proctor, born and bred. His old life, heart and soul, were buried beneath the stone that bore the name of Mason Jansen. He said nothing and did not turn back as he walked to his rented car.

# 9
# *THE OLDEST MAN*

 The idea was to find the oldest person in Jackson Hole and interview him or her about the early days when the area was a hard-to-reach, isolated backwater, snowbound in winter and barely accessible except through precarious mountain trails in summer.

It also tied in with the mountain-men promotion, which celebrated the days in the early 1800s, when trappers braved the rough climate and uncharted byways of the Rockies, lived off the land, and roamed the area in search of beaver pelts.

Always eager to focus regional and national attention on Jackson Hole, the local Chamber of Commerce championed the idea and joined with the Historical Society and the Teton County Public Library to promote the concept with various exhibits and lectures. After all, Jackson Hole had a colorful history that began when courageous indigenous people trekked over its forbidding mountain passes, followed by the intrepid mountain men who trapped beavers for their coveted under pelts during the heyday of the beaver hat. The era ended abruptly in the 1840s when silk became the new material of choice for head adornment.

Surveyors, geologists and other scientists were the next wave probing the Earth's skin and setting the stage for creation of the world's first national park, Yellowstone.

After them came the hardy band of homesteaders and the first cattle, in the 1880s. With them came the cowboys and the horse thieves who made the area their headquarters at the turn of the century. Later came European hunters looking for trophy heads of grizzlies, elk, antelope, moose and the occasional bison still left after the massive post Civil War slaughter of the breed.

Early in the century, old moneyed families from America and Europe bought large tracts of the high valley for family recreation. Then came the dude-ranch operators looking to provide a Western experience to Eastern tenderfoots. And John D. Rockfeller Jr. secretly bought up large blocks of valley land, determined to keep it out of the hands of developers, and eventually donating his 30,000-plus acres to the government to expand the reaches of Grand Teton National Park.

Now, of course, Jackson Hole is fair game for tourists, land speculators, resort operators and wealthy Americans fleeing crime-infested cities to what all agree might be the last good place on the planet. Here, the air is still crisp and clean, the landscape spectacular, and private development is allowed on only three percent of the land.

Naturally, local merchants and others with a profit ax to grind love the idea of promoting Jackson Hole, especially the Western angle, with its romantic legends of Indians, mountain men and cowboys. Never mind that the place was too cold for Indians in winter, that the mountain men disappeared when the beaver demand ended, and the cowboys came after the romantic era of gunslinging was fading fast.

Creative and tireless in their efforts to expand commerce and jingle cash registers, business boosters loved the idea of building a promotion around the oldest living person in Jackson Hole. Someone who actually had lived through the area's relatively short history and who could remember the early days would be a boon to reinforcing the romantic image of the area as a true Western historical relic.

What was needed was someone whose mind was still sharp enough to be able to recall memories of the old days and communicate them to an audience. The public-relations plan was to interview this person before a live audience and preserve the results for use in all media, print, video tape, CD-ROM and whatever else might disseminate the live message of Jackson Hole's early history. Everyone agreed that it was one helluva idea.

A committee formed to interview prospects, and the media was contacted to send out the word via newspapers, radio, television and word of mouth. The objective was to find someone who was 100 years old or more who still could recall memories of the early part of the century.

A logical place to find old residents was the Pioneer Homestead Retirement Home which housed 40 old-timers, three of whom were more than 100 years old.

Committee chairman Jack Parsons, a part owner of a catering business and a former disc jockey for a Baltimore radio station, interviewed the three candidates. They were all women. Unfortunately, one had Alzheimers, one was stone deaf and the third, while a possibility, was too frail to be moved.

"If we can't find anyone else," Jack told the committee, "we may have to lower our sights to someone younger."

"It wouldn't have the same impact," Helen Fikes said. She owned a liquor store in town. "We said 100. Let's keep looking."

"We can always lie," Harry Martin said. He owned a fudge shop in Teton Village. "Half the births of some of those old-timers were inaccurately reported."

"We said 100," Jack said. "Let's not give up just yet."

He was right. Not long after the meeting, he got a call from one of the forest rangers assigned to the Gros Ventre area of Bridger-Teton National Forest. The Gros Ventre is one of a string of mountains that partially encircles the high mountain valley of Jackson Hole. It is the only range in the lower forty eight that runs east to west instead of north to south. Gros Ventre means "big belly", a name allegedly given to it by early French beaver trappers.

"Fellow in a cabin about ten miles deep in the Gros Ventre is about what you might be looking for."

"How old?"

"Nobody knows for sure. Says he was born in 1894."

"Makes him 103."

"Lives alone. We sort of look after him."

"How long has this been going on?"

"As long as anyone in the service can remember. He's kind of like a pet. We donate old clothes, cans of chow and evaporated milk and stop by every month or so in the good weather. In winter, we can't get in."

"You mean he's 103 and lives alone? During the winter?"

"We check him out every spring, always expecting we'd find a frozen corpse. But there he is, spry as ever. It's government land and he's sort of a squatter, but we look the other way. Built this tiny cabin near a pond, God knows how many years ago. I guess you might say we grandfathered him in. He says he's lived in the cabin since the Kelly flood displaced an earlier residence."

"We're talking nearly seventy years," Jack said, not quite sure of the dates, but remembering that it was sometime in the late twenties when the Kelly flood devastated the area.

"Twenty seven," the ranger said.

"Has he got all his marbles?"

"Seems to. He also looks the part. White beard, rough clothes, looks like an old mountain man. Cabin filled with old junk. Has a potbellied stove. Mostly he lives off the land and what we give him. Used to trap and shoot game for food but his old traps are rusted out and we think he ran out of ammo for his old hunting rifle years ago."

"Sounds like our man," Jack said.

"That's what I thought," the ranger replied.

"Can you take me up to his cabin?"

"Got to go in by horse. It's pretty high."

"Will you get any flack for this?" Jack asked. "I mean, it is government land and all."

"Hell, it's one of those open secrets. He's been there seventy five years at least. Actually it's probably a good thing to call attention to him. He's really getting too old to play the mountain-man hermit. In fact, he's long past being too old."

"Sounds like he has a great story. Hell, if he's still got his marbles, he can really tell us about the old days. There were no white settlers in the valley until 1894. If he's 103, he's seen it all."

"I thought you fellows would be interested."

Jack arranged to meet the ranger at the Slide Lake overlook above Kelly the next day. The ranger told Jack that he would borrow a couple of horses from the Gros Ventre Dude Ranch nearby and they'd head up by pickup and horse trailer to what passed as a trailhead leading to the old man's cabin.

"I think we got our man," Jack told the committee when it met that evening, recounting his conversation with the ranger.

"Are you sure he's not pulling our leg?" one of the committee members asked. "It's a tough one to swallow. A man that age living alone through the winter months. He must be made of iron."

"Believe me," Jack said. "I'm going to check this out with a jaundiced eye."

"Take a camera," one of the committee members said.

As arranged, Jack met the ranger who was waiting in his old Ford pickup. He wasn't in his ranger's uniform, which meant that he was not here on official business. A horse trailer with two horses inside was attached to the pickup. The man's name was Bob Clark, and as they headed deeper into the forest of the Gros Ventre, they discussed the man they were going to see.

"I hope he's everything you said he was," Jack said. "We've got some skeptics on the committee."

"You're about to see for yourself."

"Hope he'll let me take a few pictures," Jack said.

They rode past the end of the asphalt road, onto a winding dirt road that took them past red hills and small valleys, climbing finally to the trailhead, which snaked upward through stands of aspens and lodgepoles.

Clark lifted saddle bags from the back of the pickup.

"Some canned goods and clothes," he said by way of explanation as he attached the saddle bags to the already saddled horses he had led out of the trailer.

They mounted the horses and rode upward for a couple of hours, over a trail that apparently didn't get much use.

"Looks like nobody ever comes this way," Jack said.

"It's unmarked and can't be found on official maps. Only people come up here are rangers on their way to the old man's cabin."

"How does he survive here in winter?" Jack said, looking up at the forbidding territory.

"Beats me."

"Has he got a name?"

"We call him Howdy Partner. That's the way he greets us. I guess the reference stuck as his nickname."

Finally, they broke into a clearing near a pond. The little cabin was a jerry-built graying hulk, made of old logs and listing like a sailboat heeling. At the edge of the clearing was an outhouse of similar construction. On one side of the cabin were the remains of a hitching post and on the ground an old, rotting saddle. Nearby were the rusting hulks of ancient traps. Firewood lay stacked awry against one of the cabin walls.

They dismounted and tied their horses to the old hitching post. Clark untied the saddle bags and threw them over his shoulders, then they headed for the cabin. But before they reached it, the door creaked open and a man emerged. He walked haltingly, bent over, supported by a gnarled wooden staff. He had a scraggly white beard, a mop of white unruly hair, and wore a faded flannel shirt, a dirty wrinkled leather coat and heavy, much-abused, old-fashioned high-top workshoes.

"Howdy partners," the man said in a slightly hoarse but strong voice.

"Howdy Howdy," Bob Clark said.

"Howdy," Jack said.

"Come to visit," Clark said. "Brought you some stuff."

"Much obliged," Howdy said.

Up close, that part of the man's face not obscured by the white beard was weathered and crisscrossed by wrinkles, but the light blue eyes, though faded and bloodshot, appeared alert and wary. When the man spoke, he showed yellowed front teeth. The teeth at the sides of his mouth were gone.

Right out of central casting, Jack thought. He had the perfect look for what the committee had in mind, a cross between a mountain man and Santa Claus.

"This here is Jack Parsons," the ranger said.

The old man nodded and ran his fingers through his beard. Jack felt himself being inspected.

"He's got a proposition for you, Howdy," Clark said, glancing at Jack.

They stood at the entrance to the cabin. The old man made no offer for them to come inside.

"You say you're 103?" Jack asked.

"What my Mama's old bible says in her writin'," the old man said. "Born in April of 1894, the writin' said."

"Think we can see that?" Jack asked.

"Got lost in the flood back in twenty-seven," the old man explained.

"What's your name?" Jack asked.

"Floyd Sampson," the old man said. He looked toward Bob Clark. "Rangers call me Howdy, but I don't mind. They're good folks. Bring me stuff."

"When was the last time you were in the town of Jackson, Floyd?"

The old man stroked his beard and pondered the question.

"Fifteen, twenty years. Used to go regular to get supplies. Was when Nelly was alive."

"Your wife?" Jack asked.

The old man chuckled.

"My mule."

Jack and Bob exchanged glances. Jack nodded. He's our man, he thought.

"Were you born in the valley?" Jack asked.

"Never been no place else. Pushed cattle on the old Holland ranch. Hunting guide some winters. Fishing guide. Odd jobs." Floyd shrugged. "After that mountain fell and the flood come, built this cabin. Stayed up here mostly. Gettin' too crowded below."

Jack again exchanged glances with Bob Clark. The trick was to find a way to get this man to Jackson for the promotion. It was obvious that money wasn't going to be much of a lure.

"You got a hell of a story to tell, Floyd Sampson," Jack said. Floyd shrugged uncomprehending.

"Story?"

"I mean to tell other people. You've been around a long time."

"Bones gettin' tired," Floyd said, offering a semblance of a smile.

Jack sized up the man. Despite his age, his mind seemed clear.

"So you've lived here in this valley all your life, Floyd?"

"Right here in Jackson's Hole."

"They call it Jackson Hole now."

"Don't care what they call it now. It's Jackson's Hole," the old man said. And a curmudgeon to boot, Jack thought.

"Tell him what you have in mind, Parsons," the ranger said.

"I got this proposition," Jack began, explaining the idea they had in mind, editing his explanation so that it would be presented more as an educational project rather than a tourist promotion. The old man listened intently, his eyes concentrated on the ground. From the old man's indifferent reaction, it didn't appear to Jack that he was making any headway.

"You understand what I'm saying?" Jack asked.

"Nothin' wrong with my hearin'," the old man said.

"Strikes me, Floyd," Jack said, trying to emulate what he imagined was the talk and tone of mountain men, "that you're getting too old to fare for yourself up here. I think I could arrange for you to go to the Pioneer Homestead Retirement Home in Jackson. Won't have to endure the hard winters. They'll take good care of you."

"I can take care of myself," Floyd muttered.

"All right, then," Jack said, wracking his brain for an idea that would bring the man down from the mountains. "If you do this for us, we'd be prepared to provide you with anything you want," Jack said. "Just name it."

The old man stroked his beard and pondered the suggestion.

"Tell you what," Floyd said. "You come on inside."

He turned and, with effort, moved slowly toward the cabin, then turned again, speaking to the ranger.

"Just this fella," Floyd said, pointing with his stick toward Jack.

The ranger nodded.

"I'll wait out here."

Jack followed him as he hobbled into the cabin. It was incredibly filthy and smelled of damp rot and urine. On one side was a bed made of rough-hewn logs and covered with a badly frazzled bear skin. Another bearskin riddled with worn patches covered a small part of the dirt floor. A board stretched over two log stumps served as a table. Another log stump served as a chair.

Clothing, most of it looking cast-off and unwashed, hung on nails hammered into the logs. Empty food cans littered one corner of the cabin. In the center of the room was a cast-iron potbellied stove and a pile of cut wood. Nowhere to be seen were books or pictures.

Floyd picked up an old rifle that was leaning against the wall. It had the look of an antique, but was surprisingly well cared for.

"If you could fix up old Betsy here," Floyd said, "I'd be obliged. Still works good but ran out of cartridges about five years ago. Good ole .33 Winchester. "Suddenly, he lowered his voice and pointed with his chin to what was unmistakably a referral to the ranger. "They warn me about shootin' game. Says somethin about needin' to get permission."

"A hunting license," Jack said.

"Didn't need no license once. Could shoot anytime, anything, anywhere. I keep askin' for bullets, only they don't oblige."

"You start shooting elk or antelope, they can haul you out of here."

"Been eatin' carrion," the old man said. "Tastes bad."

Jack observed what seemed like a wink offered by the old man.

"I'll come down, if'n you get me them 33s for old Betsy. She been pretty good to me over the years. Done the job."

Jack took the rifle and inspected it."

"What's that brand again?"

"Winchester 33"

"I'll check with the gunsmiths in town and see how I can get you what you want." He inspected the rifle so as to convey the correct information to a gunsmith.

"You ain't gonna say nothin' to them?" the old man said, pointing again with his chin.

"Word of honor," Jack said, wondering if it was possible to get cartridges for such an ancient weapon. "You have to promise that you'll get a hunting license."

The old man nodded, but Jack felt somehow that the man's nod was less than sincere.

"If I can't find it, I think I can get the committee to get a brand new hunting rifle."

"Don't want no new rifle. I just want old Betsy to work again."

Jack pondered the idea for a few moments. He vowed to himself to do his best to find bullets for the old Winchester. It would, he decided, be a private thing. There was no need for the committee to know anything about the transaction.

"I don't tell nobody, you don't tell nobody," Jack said.

The old man nodded.

"You come up here with them cartridges and I go down there."

It was, of course, a gamble. But encouraged by the possibility, Jack asked the old man if he could take a few pictures. He followed the old man outside and shot some pictures. Then they said goodbye.

"What was that all about?" the ranger asked when they had mounted the horses and waved a final farewell to the old man.

"I think he'll do it," Jack said. "Crazy old coot."

"What would be the trade-off?"

"He may be interested in that old-age home," Jack lied after a long pause. The ranger looked at him and frowned, obviously not believing his explanation. Then they moved out of the clearing and into the forest for the downward journey. When they got to the trailhead, they put the horses in the trailer and headed back to the Kelly slide.

"We sure appreciate this," Jack said to the ranger, shaking his hand and getting into his car for the trip back to Jackson.

"Don't know how you did it," the ranger said. "You must be one helluva salesman.

When he got back to town, Jack went immediately to one of the gunsmith shops and asked the owner if it was possible to obtain the ammunition for an old Winchester 33. Jack guessed its age as having been purchased sometime before the beginning of World War I.

"Thirty-threes," the gun dealer pondered. "I think I might be able to find something that might work."

On that promise, Jack told the committee about his luck in getting the old man to come down off the mountain. He developed the pictures and had them enlarged, then passed them around to committee members.

"I don't believe it," Helen Fikes said.

"It'll get national publicity," Elmer Borne said.

"Make a helluva poster," Al Halloway added.

They all agreed, and a large poster of Floyd was made to announce the event with the slogan "A Hundred Years in Jackson Hole by an Eyewitness." The local papers carried pictures of the old man, describing him as the oldest living Jackson Holer and the last of the authentic mountain men, which was less than accurate but certainly romantic. As predicted, the story stimulated national interest.

Jack got the cartridges to fit the old Winchester and, on the morning of the event, rode one horse up and led another by rope to the old man's cabin. He did not want to get the ranger involved. Throughout the upward ride, Jack worried that the old man had forgotten his promise, but was encouraged when the old man stepped out of his cabin and waved.

"Howdy Partner," the old man said.

After a couple of "Howdy Howdies," Jack gave the man a box of ammunition, then followed him into the cabin. It smelled just as awful as before. The old man took the rifle outside, filled its single chamber, sited and aimed at a nearby tree. A shot boomed out and hit the tree. The old man smiled, showing his yellow teeth.

"Can we go now?" Jack asked.

"Only if I take old Betsy," the old man said.

"Do you have to?"

"Now that she's workin."

It was too late to risk protest, so Jack helped the old man onto the horse and, holding the rope, led the horse down to the trailhead. He loaded the horses into the trailer, dropped them off at the dude ranch and headed back to Jackson.

Floyd said little during the journey, although he did seem interested in the changing face of the valley landscape. He smelled badly, and Jack had to keep the windows of his Suburban wide open to get relief.

"A lot different when you grew up here, wasn't it, Floyd?"

"Mountains are still here," Floyd said, then grew silent.

Jack's plan was to check into the Snow King hotel, get Floyd cleaned up, then baby-sit him until the show was to begin. Walking through the lobby, heads turned to see the old man in the white beard and rough clothes, holding his rifle in one hand and his walking stick in the other.

"Must be a costume party somewhere," Jack heard a tourist say. Those that tried to get too close quickly retreated. Inside the hotel room, Jack showed him the bathroom and demonstrated the plumbing appliances for the old man.

"I'll just wait outside in the bedroom until you take a bath," Jack said, closing the door behind him. The old man opened it a moment later.

"Don't need no bath," he said.

"Really, Floyd, it would be a good idea. You do smell a bit gamey."

"Was in the pond last moon," Floyd said.

"Last moon?"

"Six, seven times a year alls I need. Clothes and all."

Grist for the mill, Jack thought. The old man sat down on the floor Indian style, cradling his rifle in his lap. In less than a minute, his head lowered to his chest and he was asleep. Jack took after-shave lotion from his kit and rubbed it over his face to help mask the smell, then went over his notes until it was time to begin the public interview.

Waking the old man, he took him downstairs and drove the short distance to the ice-skating rink. Beside the rink was a large meeting room, crowded now. Every seat was taken and there was standing room four deep at the back of the room. Several television cameras had been set up, and there was a nest of microphones on a table at the front of the room.

"Great crowd, Jack," Helen Fikes, who was going to introduce Jack and the old man, said as they came through the center of the room, the old man leaning on his stick and carrying old Betsy.

"God, does he smell bad, Jack," Helen whispered.

"Gives him a more authentic aura," Jack said mischievously. He was getting used to the smell.

Helen then made her introduction to the now-hushed audience. Jack had written it, describing the old man as an authentic mountain man who was, as far as they knew, the oldest person in the valley. Jack had sketched in what he had learned about the old man, calling him one of the original early cowboys and fishing and hunting guides, embellishing and romanticizing the old man's background, including calling him one of the first white men born in the valley, which might be true, although the chances were that his birth had never been recorded.

Helen recounted, reading from Jack's introduction, that the old man had lived in Kelly before the flood, knew every inch of the valley floor and had climbed the Teton, Gros Ventre and Wind River mountain ranges and explored all of the seven national forests that surrounded the area. It was a stirring introduction, and it primed the audience for what was to come.

The old man listened impassively as if he were uncertain who the woman was talking about. During her remarks, the old man nodded off, and Jack had to prod him in the ribs to wake him. The audience was awed into absolute silence by Helen's remarks, especially when she told them that he had lived in the Gros Ventre wilderness in a cabin built with his own hands for seventy-odd years, surviving the harsh winters and living off the land, an authentic mountain man.

She lauded Jack, also according to what he himself had written, and thanked the ranger, who also was present, for bringing the old man's whereabouts to their attention.

After a long round of applause, Jack took the microphone and introduced the old man, who seemed to have reached full alertness by the loud enthusiasm of the applause. Starting at the beginning, Jack elicited from the old man all the vital statistics in his memory. According to his mother's bible, his father had died in 1894, the same year he was born.

"How did he die?" Jack asked.

"Fell off his horse whilst drunk," the old man said, getting a laugh.

Jack got the old man to tell them about his early life, wrangling horses for old man Holland, who brought the first herd of cows into the valley, fishing the Snake, the Green, the Gros Ventre. No fish less than two feet, the old man said, showing the length with his arms. He told of hunting bear, elk, antelope, moose and bison and talked about the snow in the valley as high as two horses standing on top of each other.

The audience listened with rapt attention. Here was oral history at its finest, a true relic of the past, someone living who could validate the early days of the valley, satisfying the craving of the audience for the real thing. Then Jack asked the question that the audience, and Jack, had been waiting to be answered.

"Tell me, Floyd, were there ever any women in your life?" Jack asked. He could hear the audience's reaction, an awesome sigh punctuated by an occasional chuckle.

"You remember women, don't you Floyd?" Jack asked. The audience broke out in sustained laughter.

"Every one," the old man answered.

"You remember their names?"

"First was Rachel. She was fourteen when she come to me. Short woman. Good teeth." The audience laughed. "Then Hanna. Part Indian. Used cow fat on her hair. Let's see now. Sarah was next. Big up front and in the rear end. Buckin' bronco that one. Tired a man out. Then Kit, then Violet, then . . . who was it? . . ." The old man pondered a moment. The audience was mesmerized into silence. "Could be Grace or Charlotte. Can't be certain for sure."

"They were your wives?" Jack asked. He too was stunned by the rendition.

"My women. Never did have a preacher."

"Were there any children?"

"Oh they did lots of birthing."

"You know how many children you fathered?"

"Twenty, twenty one. Forgit."

Jack looked into the faces of the perplexed audience. He could actually hear the people breathing for the silence.

"Do you still see any of your wives, Floyd?"

"Nope."

"You know where they are?"

"Yup. Sure do."

Jack wasn't sure where the interview was going now. If this fellow was telling them a pack of lies, then the entire credibility of the interview was going down the drain. Authenticity was at stake. He looked helplessly at Helen Fikes and felt a river of sweat sliding down his back.

"Do they ever try and contact you?"

The old man scratched his head and smiled his yellow-tooth smile.

"Caint. They're all dead. Kids, too."

"How awful," Jack said, a sinking feeling in the hollow of his stomach. "Having such bad luck."

"Wasn't bad luck," the old man said. "It was good shootin' with Betsy here." He lifted the rifle that had been on his lap.

The audience began to fidget with anxiety. Jack was stunned by the assertion. This definitely was not what he expected. This old man was a damned liar, and the reason he didn't seem to be 103 years old was because he wasn't. Nevertheless, Jack knew he had to question the man further. There was no going back. Not now.

"Are we being led to understand that you shot your wives to death?"

"All except Sara, who died natural," the old man said.

"And the children?"

"Had to. Couldn't feed 'em through the winter up there. Let the women keep them up until the milk run out."

"Then you shot them?"

Jack could hardly speak. He turned to the audience.

"I don't believe this for a minute," he told them.

"I give 'em no pain. None of them. Not animals, either. Shoot 'em right straight in the heart. I bury them all real Christian with words I remembered from my Mama's old bible."

"You can't expect us to believe this," Jack said.

"No matter. Half of them's graves got washed away in the flood. Then when I built my cabin, I come down to the valley and bring them up one at a time. Can't handle two. Never could. Belly achin' all day and all night."

"How did you get them to come with you?"

"Promises," the old man said. "I kept 'em, too. Treated 'em all real good."

"You said you shot them, Floyd."

"Had to. No way I could feed 'em through the winter. Not up there. But while they was around, I showed them the good life. Did my duty by them."

"And after . . . "Jack began, pausing. He decided to turn the interview into a spoof and started to mug for the audience, winking, raising his eyebrows, grimacing and shaking his head in gestures of incredulousness. Soon the audience began to laugh at the old man's responses.

"Buried 'em. Like I told you. Got a nice little cemetery up about a quarter mile from my camp. Give each one a stone in which I carved their names. All in heaven now cause they got a good Christian burial."

The audience listened, uttering sporadic nervous laughter. Jack could see they still wanted more.

"When was the last of them?"

The old man looked at the ceiling for a minute.

"Fifty years, maybe," Floyd said. "Got to be too much trouble." He patted his rifle. "Betsy done the job. I wouldn't do it any other way. Got so I didn't like all that woman jabbering. Got to like bein' on my own."

"Fifty years without a woman," Jack said, offering the audience what he hoped would be a mock look of disbelief and lasciviousness.

"Lucky you," one of the wags in the audience shouted. The spectators laughed.

"You felt no remorse for these acts of killing?" Jack asked, hoping the audience would see the comedy in it.

"What's that?" the old man asked.

"Did you feel sorry for them?"

The old man scratched his head.

"Nope. I did them a favor. Winters are real cold up there. Weren't enough food or clothes. Nothing worse than dyin' of frost bite. I did them good."

"By killing them?" Jack asked.

"Put 'em in heaven, I did. They wuz all good folks. Lot warmer in heaven."

Jack turned toward the audience.

"It's all spontaneous and unrehearsed, folks," Jack said.

"Where'd you find this actor, Jack?" Helen Fikes said into the microphone.

"He's right out of central casting," Jack said. "I thought you'd be amused."

The audience applauded, and Jack and the old man walked to a side door where the Suburban was parked.

"You sure fooled me," Jack said, as he drove back to the hotel.

"'Bout what?" the old man asked.

"Telling people that you killed those women and children," Jack said. "Talk about tall stories."

"But I did, like I tole you and them folks."

"You're full of bull, old man," Jack said.

The telephone rang almost when they had arrived. It was Helen Fikes.

"They loved it Jack," she said. "You had us all fooled. It was great entertainment."

After he hung up, the ranger called.

"I'll be going up to the cabin with you in the morning. The sheriff, too."

"You believe him?"

"I can tell you more about animals than people, Jack."

Jack instructed the operator to put no more calls through and barely managed to get more than a few hours sleep. As a precaution, he took old Betsy, which the old man had placed beside him on the floor, emptied the chamber and slipped the box of bullets from the old man's pocket.

Jack managed to get through the night. By pouring his bottle of after-shave over his pillow, he managed to mask the smell, but his mind wouldn't let him believe that the old man had killed all those people.

Of course, he thought, if it was true, it might actually be the best possible publicity for the valley. Floyd would be a celebrity and, in today's world, "celebrity" was all that mattered to capture people's interest. They'd call the old man the Bluebeard of Jackson Hole and the man would become an instant worldwide phenomena. It would be the truest story of them all, not just the stuff of imagined legend grown stale with age.

They moved up the Gros Ventre range that morning in a five-horse caravan, the ranger leading the way, followed by Jack, the old man, the Teton County sheriff and one of the sheriff's men leading a mule laden with picks and shovels.

When they got to the old man's cabin, Jacked helped him off his horse.

"OK, Floyd," Jack said. "Moment of truth. Where is this cemetery you talked about?

"Yonder," the old man pointed with his walking stick.

He started to walk behind the cabin and they followed him through a stand of lodgepoles to a clearing.

"Jesus," the sheriff said, shaking his head as he viewed the neat rows of flat stones that served as grave markers. Jack counted twenty-three.

"I don't believe this," the sheriff said. "And there's no statute of limitations on murder."

Despite the ghoulishness of the situation, Jack was elated by the prospect of publicity. This could go on for years, he thought.

"Least we could do is confirm that there are bones under there," the sheriff said, talking to his man. He put his shovel in the ground and started to dig. They all watched as the sheriff's man removed shovels full of earth from the area under the first stone. Nobody spoke as they watched the man dig deeper into the ground.

"Don't know what you're doin' that for," the old man said.

Without answering, they watched the sheriff's man do his grim work.

"Hit something," he said, then jumped into the shallow hole. He had gone down about three feet. He fiddled in the dirt with his hand and brought up what looked like a piece of bone. He lifted it and showed it around.

"Looks like a femur," the ranger said.

"So it wasn't a pack of lies," the sheriff said, lifting the brim of his hat with one finger.

"I told you," the old man said. "Don't know why you're doing this. I told you. I don't lie."

The sheriff turned to the old man.

"How many did you do before the flood?"

The old man looked up at the sky as if he might find the answer there.

"'Bout the same."

"Nearly fifty?"

"Bout," the old man said.

The men stood around the exposed hole. Nobody said anything for a long time. The reality of this mass murder had stunned them into silence. Jack studied the old man's face, looking for the slightest sign of remorse or contrition. I le saw none. To him, committing these murders was as natural as the rhythmical flow of the seasons.

"It's a helluva story," Jack said finally, sensing in himself a terrible conflict of mixed emotions. "We won't need any more tourist promotions, that's for sure." He couldn't wait to tell the committee.

"Put him away for life at least," the sheriff's man said, resuming his shoveling. The men chuckled at the joke.

# 10
## FLY FISHING

The boy cast over the spot where he had seen the trout's brief rise, the line arcing, swift and silent, the fly's fall gentle, landing like a tiny parachute. The father cast farther to the right, giving the boy's line enough clearance for a potential strike. So far that morning, the boy, whose name was George, had lost two cutthroat, one where a line had snagged on an unseen rock and another that had fought hard enough to tear the fly from the leader.

If it had depressed the boy, he hadn't shown it, shrugging in that half-comical way he had, using his favorite word of derision.

"Shoot."

"There's plenty more," the father, Gary, said, smiling, tousling the boy's blonde hair, bleached toe-head from the bright summer Wyoming sun. The boat floated gently on the smooth river tide under a cloudless blue sky. Father and son both loved that Green River, flowing high through ranch country. In the distance on both sides, they could see cattle grazing.

This had been a regular routine since the boy was five years old, and his father had taught him the elements of fly-fishing—the cast, the flies, how to read the river waters. They had fished all the rivers within reach—the Snake, the Green, the Gros Ventre, the Salt, the South Fork, Henry's Fork and others.

The boy was fourteen now and surpassed the father in the skill of the cast. He had even begun to tie his own flies and could knot a fly to the leader in the flash of an eye.

The routine of these father-son exhibitions was unfailingly rhythmical in its ritual; the preparation the night before, assembling their tackle boxes and flies and checking reels, lines, leaders, spares and waders, hats, sun lotion, sunglasses, vests. Mariam made sure the lunch was packed with favorites, overstuffed deli-sandwiches, the thermos of coffee and cans of soda, and the usual array of junk foods, always including chips and Milky Way candy bars.

For Gary, this was dad-and-son nirvana, perhaps an overcompensation for what he had not gotten from his own father, leaving that big hollow in his heart. Gary had imagined his dad would have done these things with him if he had made it through Vietnam. Now he was an engraved name on the War Monument in Washington, a framed rubbing of that name in their living room and a gravesite with a cross in a government cemetery in California.

There also was the ritual of Mariam's goodbye—the kisses and hugs for both of them and the usual "be carefuls." Today, the little loving ritual was for George alone. She had merely nodded his way, her glance cold and disinterested.

Mariam had never gone with them out of conviction that

this was a father-son thing, a verboten area for her and Amy, their daughter, who apparently understood. With Amy, it was more a horse-riding adventure, which was done mostly with Mariam, although Gary went sometimes.

"Strike!" George shouted, feeling the pull on the line.

"A biggie," Gary said, observing the line's angle and calculating the trout's weight.

The boy waited as the fish tugged, deepening the hook, then took a turn on the reel to give the trout a clue as to the dominance of the fisherman. The line rolled out, George letting the trout understand he was having his way, making sure the hook was deep enough now.

Gary held back any advice. The boy knew exactly how to perform, judging the weight on the line, the swiftness of the movement below, and how much line would be needed to bring the cutthroat to the boat.

He observed the boy's sure movements, watched his face through the opaqueness of his tear-glazed eyes. He could see the boy's expression, joyful with victory and concentration, as he reeled in the line at intervals, fighting the cutthroat, watching the line cut through the water sideways, first to one side, then the other.

"Got you sucker," the boy said, respecting the fish's maneuver and his fighting spirit as he had been taught. They were pugilists of the river. In the end, there would be for a brief moment only victor and vanquished, but always comrades joined in elegant and temporary combat.

Gary reeled in to watch the boy and trout battle to the finish. He was happy for the boy, whose past disappointments this day—losing the two fish—disappeared in the joy of this new enterprise of battle. After the placement of the fly and the strike, the fight was everything, a battle for glory between species.

The boy looked up happy, glancing at his father, who smiled back and nodded his approval. The boy smiled with pride. The line suddenly went dead, but the boy knew that the fish was still on the hook.

"Playing possum," the boy said. "Won't help."

The boy reeled in more line and the fish got the message, and with a strong flourish, it zipped away again, forcing the boy to let out more line. Gary could tell that the fish was recognizing the futility of escape and losing his appeal and energy for the fight. The boy reeled in more line, not stopping now. Both father and son peered over the boat's side into the river. Below, they could see the fish, the hook still impaled in his mouth. He looked sleek and, despite his situation, proud and unbowed.

"Five pounds at least," Gary said.

"More like ten," George replied.

"Never was a good judge of pound," Gary said, touching the boy's back, more like a caress than a pat. The boy got his net and scooped the fish out of the water.

"A beaut, son," Gary said.

The boy dipped his hand into the net and picked up the fish, holding its gills closed to keep it from wriggling free. Gary had whipped out his pocket camera, and the boy grinned as he held up the fish for the picture. Then the boy kneeled and, with both hands, gently placed the fish back into the water.

"So long, pal," the boy said as the fish waited for his recent trauma to dissipate, then moved slowly away from the boat. "I'll be seeing you again, fella."

He turned to Gary, who noted that the boy's expression had turned dark.

"You too, dad," the boy said.

"We've been through that son," Gary said, clearing his throat as if to chase the sob that lingered there.

"It sure won't be the same."

"Things change, George. That's the only thing you can bank on."

The boat continued its gentle float downriver, but the boy made no move to pick up his reel and cast. Gary made one long cast, then reeled in. He suddenly had lost his enthusiasm for the day's sport.

"Hungry?" he asked his son.

The boy shrugged, expressing his indifference. Gary took the oars and glided the boat to shore, jumping onto the grass and bringing the boat's prow to rest on solid ground. The boy got the pack that contained the food and hefted it to the grass, then jumped to solid ground himself. He watched while his father set the sandwiches and the drinks on a checkered tablecloth that Mariam had provided.

They sat Indian style by the side of the tablecloth. Gary unwrapped the sandwiches and flipped open the canned drinks. The boy looked at his sandwich in disgust, then put it back on the paper plate.

"I can't eat," he said.

"Your mother went to a great deal of trouble. . . ."

"I'm really impressed . . . with both of you."

"Look son, we've been through it. It wasn't my fault."

"It had to be," George said. "Mom wouldn't have done it on her own."

"She didn't, son. She just . . . well . . . I don't know how to put it so you'll understand." Gary couldn't control the sob now and let it out, turning away. He did not want the boy to see the sudden gush of tears. Calming, he turned back to the boy. "These things happen. She fell in love with someone else is all. Simple as that. She's a good and honest woman. She was not unfaithful and she followed her heart. People do that in life."

"I don't care what other people do," the boy said, pouting.

"You're still my son, and I love you."

"You let it happen. You didn't fight hard enough."

"I fought with everything I had," Gary said.

"No, you didn't," the boy said. He slapped his fist down on the tablecloth, bunching it. One of the soda cans fell and liquid poured out on the cloth.

"Look what you did," Gary said, picking up the can and moving it to the grass.

"You let it happen," the boy said.

"I didn't," he protested, wondering if the boy had a point. Mariam had been Jack Donnely's dental assistant for two years. That it was anything more than a job never crossed his mind. In retrospect, he had seen signs—a subtle physical withdrawal, a lessening of verbal terms of endearment, an accelerating sense of toleration, a growing noninvolvement.

Perhaps he had been too worried about his own situation. The valley construction business had slowed and with it had come an architectural depression. He hadn't had a house to design in two months and had begun to think of moving on. An offer had come from a school chum in Kansas City and, so far, he had declined.

He had broached such a possibility to Mariam who had been adamant in her objection. Of course, he hadn't known then about her secret agenda. Besides, she was a native, granddaughter of homesteaders, and this valley was her world. He had decided finally to tough it out.

Then, out of the blue two weeks ago had come this heart-stopping confession. It left him stunned. In fact, he was still in shock.

"I am in love with another man," she had told him, identifying her boss. "I swear to you that I have not been unfaithful in a physical sense. But I need this man, and I want a divorce so I can marry him." There was more, of course, but after that his mind had lost its comprehension.

Gary was too traumatized to make a rational comment. It was as if his tongue had frozen in his mouth. He left the house and walked a few miles along the river dike, nursing his self-pity, before he could summon the courage to return.

By then the children had gone to bed and Mariam was sitting up reading a novel. He remembered wondering how it was possible for her to concentrate after such a momentous and unnerving confession. It was then that he realized that for her it was an unburdening. She was relieved. He was the only one of the two who was truly pained and badly wounded.

"You're serious, then?" he asked, crawling in bed beside her, as if nothing was amiss in their relationship. She made no objection, lying stiffly beside him.

"Absolutely," she replied.

"Just like that?" he asked.

"The shortest distance between truths is a straight line," she said, taking off her reading glasses, closing the book and placing it on the night table. Her explanation seemed rehearsed, as if she had worked on every word for a long time.

"And how long has this little love-fest been going on?"

"Long enough."

"While you've been playing the devoted wife and mother?"

"I was hoping to avoid acrimony," she sighed.

"Were you expecting approval, consent, agreement? Mariam, you've just axed my life. Avoid acrimony? Am I made of stone? I've been betrayed, lied to. You've lived with me under false pretenses."

"I know, and I feel awful about that part. Most of our life together has been good and we have two wonderful children.

Whatever you think about me, I ask you to please think of them."

"As if I don't," Gary said, simmering, keeping his voice modulated so as not to be heard by the sleeping children.

"Believe me, I know how you must feel. Sometimes to save yourself, you have to be cruel. Don't make it more difficult for me. I'm ready to compromise on everything."

"I hope you haven't told the kids yet," Gary said, suddenly panicked.

"I guess we've got to make that a joint effort."

"It won't be easy for them, Gary, and I hope you will agree to a very minimum of disruption for them."

He noted the precision of her words. She had never been that concise. Or cold. His mind had searched for ways to dissuade her but he could sense that it was hopeless and he had too much pride to be a beggar. He had always believed that theirs was a good marriage that had grown from passionate love to respect and mutual interest. They were good and devoted, loving parents. That such a thing could happen was beyond his comprehension. It suddenly occurred to him that Jack Donnely also had a family.

"Jack has told Amy," Mariam said, as if she was reading his mind.

"And what, pray tell, will be their arrangement?" he said, grappling with his anger and unable to control his sarcasm.

"Amy will get the house," she said. "I hope you will agree to that for me. My parents will help me buy out your end."

"They know?" he asked. He felt even more humiliated. How long had they known?

"Of course, they're not happy about it. Who could be?"

"You are."

"Please, Gary, don't make it messy. That's all I ask. For me, for you and especially for the children."

"So I'm supposed to lose my house."

"Not lose. Sell. We're going to buy you out."

"And the kids? Do I lose them, too? Or do you plan to buy them too?"

"This is too serious to be facetious about, Gary. Neither Jack nor you will be deprived of access to the children."

"Access?" Gary asked. "Access?" He raised his voice. "You use such a word to describe a father's relationship with his children. Access?"

He sprang out of bed. This was ridiculous, he thought, lying in bed with this woman who had betrayed him in the worst possible way. No, he decided, she had not been faithful, despite her protestations. How could one believe her after so much dissimulation. Who knows how long she had been wearing this disguise. Never would he ever get back in that bed. Never. He felt his heart pounding in his chest.

"How else could I describe it? I know how the kids feel about you. I would want no impediments to your seeing them. . . ." She paused for a few moments, watching him pace the room, staying calm under the quilt of their once joint bed. She was still a pretty woman and he had loved her passionately. Perhaps he still did. It was a burden he did not want to carry.

"Am I supposed to be grateful?" he asked.

"Not grateful, Gary. Understanding. I know you'll do the right thing about child support as well."

It was another issue that he hadn't contemplated. He had been living on bank loans, waiting for the next job to happen. During such lean times, Mariam had always been supportive and they had weathered the storms. This was different. How could he possibly live in a town with another man heading his family, sitting in his chair at the head of the table, sleeping with his wife, playing dad to his kids.

"I'll probably take that Kansas offer," he said, sensing the full weight of his defeat.

"Your choice, Gary. But it probably makes sense."

"Nothing makes sense, Mariam. Nothing."

The conversation replayed in his mind as he watched the boy express his frustration and anger.

"You let it happen," the boy repeated.

"Don't do this, George," Gary said. "No matter what, I'm still your dad. I love you with every ounce of my being. Surely you know that. I didn't want this."

"Shoot," the boy said.

"I'll come visit often and you'll spend time with me in Kansas. Maybe summers. We'll go fishing in Kansas. There are rivers there too."

"Not like these."

"How could you know that?"

"I just know it." He took a bite of sandwich and tried chewing, then spit it out.

"And I'll come back to Jackson Hole. Hell, son, it's not the end of the world."

"It is for me."

"Your Mom loves you and Amy, George. She won't let you down. You know that."

"It'll never be the same. Never."

The boy got up and walked toward a clump of bushes making as if he were going to relieve himself. Gary knew better. He could see his son's shoulders begin to shake and he knew he was crying, crying bitterly, with every fiber of his being. Then, he too, walked to another part of the area and collapsed against a tree, unable to hold back his tears of pain and hysteria.

It would never be the same, he knew. Never. There would be other fly-fishing trips, of course, but they would never

ever be the way it had been. The ritual of the night before, the getting ready part, the choice of flies, the checking of the reels and lines, the taste of the those deli sandwiches made in that special way, the farewell hug and kiss from Mariam. Then there was the drive through misty or sunny mornings to the river, the smell of it, the reading of the river and the hatch, the casting of the lines, the strike, the fight, the victory or loss, and the gentle return of the fish to the river.

And the loving bonds created between father and son. Oh, God, how this will be missed. He stood up, took some deep breaths, then turned and started back to where he had laid out the tablecloth.

His son was standing at the river's edge now, pole and reel in hand. Yet he did not appear to be getting ready to cast. Nor would it have been a clear shot. Then, suddenly, as if he were flinging a javelin, the boy flung the equipment into the river.

"George!" Gary cried, running toward the river's edge.

The boy did not turn. He simply stood there, watching the equipment float downstream and disappear from sight. Gary touched the boy's shoulders and the boy turned and fell, sobbing, into his father's arms.

They stood there for a long time, locked in a tight embrace. Then they headed home.

# 11
# THE DRESS

Maggie rolled down the last leg of Teton Pass feeling a sense of elation she hadn't felt for a long time. There, beneath her, was her beautiful valley, a palette of mustard hues flecked with green in the late-afternoon June sun.

But it was not simply the beauty of the valley that filled her heart with such upbeat emotion. She had found Francie the most wonderful party dress for the manageable price of $32 at Mrs. Ramsay's place in Driggs. It was a full-skirted peasant dress with cumberbund and matching pastel flowers embroidered on the skirt.

Mrs. Ramsay, a nice Mormon lady, sold secondhand clothes from her little house in Driggs. It was a find, a really lucky find. Maggie had gotten her name out of the Driggs classifieds. She often shopped in Driggs, especially at Thriftway, where the prices were a lot less than at Albertsons, which now, owing to some incompetent political judgments, had a virtual monopoly in Jackson.

Of course, if you added on the gas and the wear and tear on her 1987 Honda, from going over the pass and all, you cut into the savings a bit. Today, Maggie refused to dwell on that subject. She was too happy. Francie would be thrilled with her purchase. It was a beautiful dress. She calculated that it would cost maybe four times as much brand new.

"Looks like it wasn't worn very much," Mrs. Ramsay told her." Maggie had inspected the garment and confirmed it. The clothes sold by Mrs. Ramsay were taken on consignment and, because of the low overhead, her clothes were a lot cheaper than the secondhand clothes sold in Jackson.

Maggie hoped Francie would be as thrilled with the dress as she was. Doug, on the other hand, would have mixed feelings. He had been laid off four weeks ago from his job as a truck driver for a cement company that had closed its doors after operating in the valley for years. The owners had pulled up stakes and gone off to Florida.

Worse, she and her husband had gotten behind in their bills and were cutting back until Doug found another job. Finances were tight. Even when Doug was working, they watched their pennies. A couple of years before, they had managed to scrape up enough money for a down payment on a house in Cottonwood Park but meeting the mortgage payments and raising three kids were a constant test of their resourcefulness.

"Count your blessings," she told Doug and her children often. "We live in this beautiful valley. There's no crime, no pollution. The schools are great and the area is an outdoor playground."

Doug loved to fish and hunt, and their freezer was well-stocked with elk, duck, rabbit and grouse that Doug had shot, butchered and dressed. Living in Jackson was a lot better than the coal-mine country of Pennsylvania, where they had both grown up. They had come here as newlyweds more than fifteen years ago, seeking a wonderful friendly place where they could enjoy the outdoors and raise a family. They had been certain that they had found it.

Maggie considered herself an optimist. On balance, she assured herself, life wasn't so bad. Everybody had their ups and downs. Even rich people. And there were plenty of rich people rolling into the valley, escaping from the big cities, looking for a place where the quality of life was better. She was not in the least bit envious.

With the exception of Doug's current situation, they had little to complain about. They were solid working people, the salt of the earth and proud of it. Maybe they had extended themselves financially, Maggie suspected, but as long as they were healthy and able to work, life was OK.

Maggie worked as a cleaning lady at $15 an hour, which she considered darn good wages for that type of work. On weekends, she worked as a waitress at the Granary, which, on good days, was worth as much as a hundred bucks, tax free. Doug, who was good with his hands, worked odd jobs after work for people who owned big houses over at Teton Pines and John Dodge.

The kids, too, helped contribute with their own after-school jobs. Francie baby-sat and Hal cut grass summers and worked winters part-time for the ski corporation. Even Matthew, who was eight, couldn't wait to get to work. There was no question in Maggie's mind that her kids somehow would get to college. All of them were smart and got outstanding grades.

The teachers at the Jackson schools were dedicated and sensitive to the needs of the kids. Francie had just graduated from the middle school and this would be her first "grown-up" party with boys at Suzie Chandler's big house in the upscale John Dodge subdivision. A number of the mothers, including herself, would be chaperones.

Maggie hadn't expected any difficulties to arise because of the party. Not that the issue blind-sided her. She had expected it to surface sooner or later. The fact was that there was an economic disparity in the school system.

More and more children of rich people were entering the system. Because there were no private nonreligious schools in the valley, the children of the so-called working class went to school with the children of parents who were moneyed and lived in big expensive houses. Sometimes, she cleaned the houses of those people whose children went to school with her kids. And Doug did odd jobs for these same people. It didn't bother Maggie, although Doug, a man of great pride, was not quite as accepting.

The problem arose when Francie came home in tears, explaining that she couldn't go to the party at the Chandlers.

"I haven't got anything to wear, Mom. Not for a party. I'll look ratty. Suzie Chandler and Alice Fox and Bobbi Taylor have beautiful clothes. I'll look awful."

Maggie understood that it was not just typical teenage imaginary angst talking. This was the real thing. Suzie Chandler, Alice Fox and Bobbi Taylor were Francie's best friends. Francie spent lots of time at Suzie's house. They kept horses and Francie had the use of them whenever Suzie and she were allowed to go riding into the forest.

Maggie felt very comfortable with Audrey Chandler. She and her husband had grown up dirt poor in Maine. Phil had built a big business in machine parts, which he had sold at a very high price, enabling them now to lead a luxurious life-style. Doug did not feel quite so comfortable with Phil

Chandler, although they did hunt elk together. As Doug explained it to Maggie, the reason for his discomfort was that Phil hunted for sport and he hunted for food.

Alice Fox and Bobbi Taylor also were from rich homes, but these were the houses where Maggie cleaned and Doug did odd jobs and, while Alice and Bobbi were devoted to Francie, Maggie could detect a sense of separation when it came to the parents. She had also heard that the Foxes and the Taylors were not entirely comfortable with having their daughters going to school with the children of parents who worked for them.

Once while she was cleaning the Foxes' house, she heard Elaine Fox say on the phone that she was considering sending Alice to a boarding school back East.

"The worst disaster," Elaine Fox had whispered into the phone, "would be if Alice falls in love with some poor working stiff and marries him. It is not an uncommon occurrence in this valley."

It wasn't as if there were open animosity between the families, and neither Alice nor Bobbi were stuck up or snobby or made Francie feel uncomfortable. Some facts, though, were inescapable. Rich kids had fancier clothes and possessions. Their parents lived in big houses, drove expensive cars, went on luxurious vacations and socialized among their peers, people with money.

It hadn't been like that during Maggie's early years in Jackson. Things were more democratic. People of all income levels socialized. There were fewer class distinctions. Now there was a gated country-club subdivision in the community and people were building bigger and bigger houses.

"Money talks and bullshit walks," Doug would say from time to time, although never in front of the children.

Nevertheless, the message never truly hit home until

Francie announced that she was not going to the party because she had nothing decent to wear.

"It's your character and personality that makes you special, honey, not your clothes."

"Sorry, Mom. But clothes are important. I don't want to go to the party looking like some hick slob."

"Hick slob? My pretty little girl. No way."

Francie was, indeed, a beautiful child, now growing into young womanhood. She was tall, blonde and graceful, and her figure had just begun to blossom. She was taking an interest in boys and they in her. She also was becoming increasingly sensitive to her family's economic situation.

"Face it, Francie," Doug told her. "We're working people. We can't compete in their league."

"I don't want to compete," Francie said, showing remnants of her little-girl whine. "All I want is a nice dress to wear. I don't want to look frumpy."

Audrey Chandler spoke to Francie one evening in the parking lot of the school after a parent/teachers meeting. Maggie sensed that she had deliberately waited until Maggie had arrived.

"Francie said she's not coming to the party, Maggie. What's going on?"

Audrey Chandler was a bright, charming, outspoken salty-tongued woman who adored Francie. There was no hint of snobbery in her demeanor. In fact, she was militantly anti-class conscious and her husband Phil was always open and friendly.

"Just teenage silliness, Audrey," Maggie said.

"Suzie says she's concerned about not having a good dress to wear," Audrey said.

"You know kids," Maggie said. Oddly, she felt a tiny tinge of embarrassment.

"Suzie will be crushed. How can she have a party without Francie?"

"I'm sure Francie will come around," Maggie muttered.

Audrey shrugged, then sucked in a deep breath.

"If it's just a dress, Francie could borrow one of Suzie's. I know a great dressmaker who could make it fit perfectly."

"I don't think Francie would go for that. I could tell you that Doug won't."

"Jesus, Maggie. The kids have been friends since first grade. Don't let stupid pride interfere. I'm sure Suzie could talk Francie into it."

"I doubt it, Audrey. Let's face it, we're the poor-but-proud group."

"God, I hate that attitude, Maggie," Audrey protested loudly. "When Hank and I got married, we didn't have a pot to piss in or a window to throw it out of. Stop this Princess-and-the-Pauper crap. Francie and Suzie love each other. Don't let anything stand in the way of that. She has got to come to the party."

"I'll talk to her," Maggie sighed.

"Insist on it, Maggie. We can't have that in this community. We are all stitched from common thread."

Maggie knew that Audrey meant what she said. There were tears in her eyes.

"Don't let this happen, Maggie," Audrey pleaded.

But nothing Maggie said could move Francie from her position. To make matters worse, Doug agreed with his daughter.

"I'm not saying that they're better than us," Doug said. "They're richer is all. They're not trapped by the lack of dough like we are."

"Don't say that, Doug," Maggie told him. "We've done a lot better than what we've come from. We've got a house, three great kids and we live in a great spot."

"And have to work our butts off to make ends meet."

"So what?" Maggie countered. "I'll tell you this. Our kids will do a heck of a lot better than we did, and we've done a lot better than our folks."

"Look at me. I'm a loser, Maggie. I just got laid off, my wife and kids have to bust their chops to keep things going and now this thing with Francie. I say let's stick to our kind, Maggie. We is "po folk." Let's not mix and mingle with the fancies."

She could see that Doug was depressed and quickly retreated. He was feeling sorry for himself and it wouldn't do to berate him when he was so fragile.

"Francie can hold her own with anyone," Maggie said, feeling a sense of militancy rise inside of her. "She's got looks and brains and maybe a little too much pride. But I'm gonna get her a smashing great dress and she's going to go to that party and hold her head up and feel like somebody."

At that moment, heading down the pass, she felt the same combativeness. We're as good as anybody, she told herself.

Since she had planned the dress as a surprise, she did not present it to Francie until after dinner. She beckoned Francie into the room she shared with her younger brother and showed her the dress.

"Oh, Mom, it's gorgeous, just gorgeous," Francie cried, putting it in front of her and looking at herself in the mirror. "Oh, Mom."

She quickly tried it on and modeled it for Maggie.

"You look like a dream, sweetheart," Maggie said through eyes filmed with tears. "My beauty."

Francie, also in tears, embraced her mother.

"I love you, Mom," she said.

"And I love you," Maggie said, insinuating herself out of her daughter's embrace. "But that's no excuse for mussing up the dress."

Maggie then helped Francie with her hair and did her face in light makeup. The objective was to show Doug and gain his acceptance and encouragement. Doug was watching a ball game when they came into the living room. It took a few moments of throat clearing and mock coughing to get his attention. When he saw his daughter modeling in front of him, he didn't quite know what to make of it.

"It's me," Francie said. "Daddy's little girl."

Doug studied her for a long moment, then frowned and shook his head as Maggie held her breath.

"Whoa there," he said. "What's this?"

"This is the dress Francie is going to wear for the party," Maggie said, with some trepidation.

"Look at her. She's only thirteen years old, for crying out loud."

Actually, the neckline was hardly too low and the skirt just the right length, but the dress revealed the outlines of Francie's growing curves and, with her hair up and makeup on, she looked older than her years.

"She's growing up, Doug," Maggie said sweetly, trying to head off his anger.

"Where the hell did you get that dress, Maggie?" Doug asked. She could tell his anger was accelerating.

"I got a great buy in Driggs," she told him. He would not have understood the concept of selling secondhand clothes on consignment. Ironically, if he had understood, he would have protested vehemently.

"You can't keep up with them, Maggie. We've been over that." He turned to his daughter. "It's a battle we can't win." He paused, his expression darkening. "I say give it back. It's a waste of money."

His conviction seemed tentative and Maggie could see that he was equally as angry with himself. He loved Francie dearly and to hurt her would be more of a trauma to himself.

"But Daddy, I love this dress. Are you saying you don't like it on me?"

"Oh Jesus, no, honey. You're the most beautiful girl in the world." He was a big man, proud in every way, with a strong sense of his masculinity and a deep love for his family. Maggie's heart was breaking for him. The truth was, for her as well, that his daughter was, indeed, growing up and the reality of her appearance carried a hint of the day she would be leaving the nest.

Without saying more, he walked out of the house. She knew, of course, that he would be out there quietly sobbing, unable to show anyone else his pain, the pain of his own perceived failure.

"You know your dad, Francie. He loves the dress on you. He just can't stand the idea of your growing up. It's not the other things, really it's not."

"Mom, I know what we can't and can afford. I'm not stupid. But because we have less money than my friends' families doesn't mean I have to look ratty."

"And you don't. You look like a movie actress, honey."

"I feel like one, Mom."

Maggie drove Francie to the party at the Chandlers' house. The Chandlers had invited a large group of kids, had hired a live band, which was already blasting away, and set up lots of food and sodas in their huge recreation room. Balloons and decorations hung from the ceiling.

"Francie," Audrey Chandler cried, kissing her. "You look like a million." Francie beamed with pride.

Maggie stood at the doorway to the recreation room watching Francie enter. She recognized most of the children from school, all at the awkward age, the boys in unaccustomed jackets and the girls in what her generation called "party" dresses. Francie, Maggie was proud to see, looked outstanding.

Watching her, she had more tolerance for Doug's reaction when he had first seen Maggie in the dress. The end of childhood was fast approaching for Francie. The thought brought tears to her eyes. Oh, God, I love you my sweet beautiful daughter, she whispered to herself.

"I love that dress," Suzie Chandler squealed as she spied Francie and ran to embrace her.

Maggie was proud to see her daughter the center of interest. She watched the party for a few moments, then realized she was not truly welcome and went into the kitchen, where Audrey was supervising her help.

"You can't imagine how glad I am that Francie could come. And that dress. It's lovely."

"Yes, it is," Maggie agreed. "It looks like you've got a great party going. Anything I can do?" It was an awkward question, in light of the fact that she sometimes was hired to help at the Chandler parties. Obviously, Audrey had decided it would be inappropriate for a mother of one of her daughter's guests to be a hired hand.

"Our job is to peek in occasionally and show parental authority, see to it that things don't get out of line."

A couple of the other mothers also were scheduled to arrive, including Sally Fox and Terri Taylor, both of whom Maggie worked for as a cleaning lady.

"Some of the dads are playing poker over at the Taylors'," Audrey said. "Keep them out of our hair."

Maggie would have loved Doug to have been invited into their game, but she knew that such a prospect was impossible and she chased such a thought from her mind, replacing it instead with the idea that she and Doug were involved in a noble task—sacrificing their own material well-being for the next generation.

Sally and Terri came through the back entrance with their daughters. The girls embraced Maggie and skipped off to join the noisy crowd of kids in the recreation room.

"Sounds like a blast," Terri Taylor said. She was an attractive blonde, dressed preppy-style with a broad smile and cute dimples.

"I wish I was thirteen again," Sally Fox said. In an odd way, although they were completely different in looks and dress, they seemed to be clones of each other.

"Not me," Audrey said. "Worrying about pimples and boys and my period. No way."

Audrey had opened a bottle of white wine and the mothers began drinking and getting chatty, starting to tell stories about their adolescent days. Both Terri and Sally were the daughters of privileged families. They talked of being pinned by fraternity boys, of formals at the country club, and of European vacations, mentioning names like Muffy and Buffy and Chub and Biff. Sometimes they communicated in slang impenetrable to Maggie's understanding, punctuated by giggles.

Nevertheless, Maggie listened to their stories feigning hilarity while their little jokes sailed over her head. The kids' party roared away at another part of the house.

"They seem to be having a fine old time," Maggie said.

"I'd love to take a peek," Sally Fox said.

Audrey gave her a platter of cookies.

"Take this in," she said, "Give us a report. They hate us staring at them during their adolescent mating rituals."

"Mating rituals?" Sally cried. "That's scary."

"It's an inevitability," Audrey sighed. "The sap is rising and those horny little devils are beginning to overflow with hormones."

Sally took the plate of cookies and, winking at the ladies, carried it in the direction of the noise.

"I guess the only thing you can count on is change," Audrey said.

Maggie agreed but made no comment. She was thinking of Francie in her beautiful dress and hoping she was having a good time.

Suddenly, Sally Fox burst into the room. Her face was ashen and there were tears in her eyes. She seemed on the verge of hysteria.

"What is it, Sally?" Audrey said.

They looked in the direction of the party. None of the children had followed her out.

"Is there something terrible going on in there?" Terri asked.

"I think we better see," Audrey said, starting in the direction of the party.

"No, please," Sally managed to say, signaling with her arms for them to stay put. She swallowed hard and wiped her tears with tissues. She looked at Maggie.

"Can you ever forgive me, Maggie?" Terri said.

"Forgive?"

Maggie was confused. Her eyes met Sally's.

"It was stupid of me," Sally said.

"For crying out loud, Sally," Audrey said. "What the hell is going on?"

"Francie's dress . . ." Sally hesitated and looked toward Maggie again. "I blurted it out. I wasn't thinking. I'm so sorry."

Maggie felt a cold chill grip her.

"What about Francie's dress?" she asked.

"I told her . . . in fact, I said it so loud. I don't know what got into me. I told them it was Alice's dress." She averted her eyes from Maggie's. "I had taken it to the lady in Driggs to sell. Alice hated it on her."

"And you told Francie?" Audrey said. "You mean they all know?"

"The whole thing was stupid," she said, turning to Maggie, sniffling but under control now. "Look, Maggie, we are rich. But don't think Hal showers me with cash. I have to make do on his budget terms. Is that a laugh?"

What about Francie?" Maggie cried. "What about my Francie?"

"It wasn't my place to stay," Sally Fox said.

Maggie and Audrey exchanged glances.

"She must be mortified," Maggie said.

"I'm so sorry, Maggie. Really I am."

"Is . . . is Francie still there?" Maggie asked tentatively. She started to move in the direction of the party. Audrey followed.

"Spoiled, dumb lady," Audrey said between clenched teeth.

They stood by the door and peeked in. The party was in full swing, the music blasting. Francie was dancing with one of the boys. The others were dancing as well, oblivious to the trauma that Sally alleged she had set in motion.

"I don't believe it," Audrey said, laughing and putting her arm around Maggie's shoulders. "Look at their dresses."

Each of the four girls who were Francie's best friends had ripped up the hems of their dresses and torn them up to their thighs. They had also stained the bodices with grape juice.

Francie spotted her mother watching them and waved, then stopped briefly from her dancing, exhibited her dress, smiled and shrugged. Maggie smiled back, shaking her head in mock rebuke. Then she mimed some words.

"You still look beautiful."

Francie waved again and turned away, returning to the rhythm of the dance.

# 12
# THE BETRAYAL

 "I've decided to stay," Maddy said.
"Stay?" Mrs. Hinton replied, looking at Mr.
Hinton. They were sitting on the patio in the soft
air of Indian summer, having their ritual before-dinner cocktail. Actually, the "cocktail" had become white wine during the last few years, ever since Mr. Hinton had vowed that he had had his last dry martini.

Even the golfers who had straggled into view during the summer twilight hours had disappeared. Most of the seasonal people had left Teton Pines and, in a few days, the Hintons would be heading back to Brentwood in Los Angeles, "two blocks from O.J." The infamous celebrity's home now was their identifying geographical beacon.

Mr. Hinton was a ruddy-faced active golfer and fly fisherman who had been born in Nebraska and made his fortune as an investment banker in Los Angeles. He was a tall, impressive, likable man with silver hair, proud of his self-made success. He had worked his way through college and Harvard Business School and now was, at sixty-two, on the cusp of retirement. Mrs. Hinton had been a school teacher but had quit in mid-career to devote herself exclusively to her three children and accommodate herself to her husband's busy schedule.

Having no distracting antecedents or social blemishes, the Hintons had been welcomed into the Los Angeles Country Club, the exclusive Jonathan Club, the Beach Club and participated in those charities that are the continuous social obligation of the Los Angeles elite. Mrs. Hinton served on two prestigious boards of charitable institutions that did good works for the disabled and the blind.

They were considered by all intelligent, caring, decent people, living examples that one can come from humble beginnings and make it to the top rung of the ladder of success. Despite the reputation of their club memberships as discriminatory and intolerant, they were encouraged by what they perceived as increasing openness in the membership-selection process.

By no means did they consider themselves bigoted or intolerant of any ethnic, religious or racial group. They respected working people and treated them with respect, alert to any conduct on their part that would attack their sense of pride and dignity.

They considered it unfortunate that working people were not among their social group, especially since they had been a part of that group in their youth. In a sense, they both agreed, they were trapped by their financial success, cast among like people who could afford their life-style of choice.

When the issue of "class" came up, they resented the suggestion that they were snobs. If there was envy of their success by the less fortunate, they dismissed it as perfectly natural. They once had felt that way themselves and made no apologies for their success and life-style. They hadn't been born with silvers spoons in their mouths but had paid their dues and earned their right to the good life.

At the same time, they recognized the growing gap between the comfortable rich and the put-upon, two-earner middle class, vividly illustrated in Jackson Hole. Although they didn't dwell on it, they were well aware of the disparity and the growing high cost of living in Jackson Hole, especially for young people just starting out.

Occasionally, they expressed their indignation over the stupidity of various acts of local politicians, especially the decision that inadvertently created a monopoly for one supermarket chain by being too tough on another chain that wished to enter the local market. Both Mr. and Mrs. Hinton viewed politicians, in general, and most representatives of the media, with suspicion.

As the Hintons said repeatedly, they knew where they came from, acknowledging that hard work and luck had won them a big piece of the American dream. Politically, they were Republicans of the moderate variety and they were Episcopalians. But they did not think of themselves as quintessential "wasps." In fact, they resented the label, although they were tolerant of the satirical references to the term.

They had visited Jackson Hole when the children were younger and it had always attracted them as a possible location for a second home for summer use. When a number of their California friends built houses there, they decided it was time to take a serious look.

They bought their lot in Teton Pines not only because it was the only spot in Jackson Hole that resembled a real country club where they could golf and play tennis, but among its members would be people of their own peer group.

They were somewhat surprised by the non-exclusivity provisions written into the club regulations at the insistence of the Teton County Commissioners. The regulations stated that anyone could dine at the club or play a round of golf if they could pay the price. Of course, they had no choice but to accept the caveat and, in time, came to support the idea as a practical matter.

Aside from the familiar ambiance of the atmosphere, they would be able to enjoy the wonderful outdoor recreation, especially the spectacular fly fishing, and, of course, the beauty and esthetics of the valley were unsurpassed. To them, it was the best of both worlds.

They built a large, beautiful five-bedroom Western-style house overlooking the 16th hole. They decorated the interiors of the house with expensive art, mostly depicting cowboys in action, wildlife and landscapes of the Rocky Mountains. They enjoyed the mythology of the West, and a number of their rooms contained original Molesworth designs.

Maddy was their youngest child, now 22. She had graduated from Wellesley with a major in child psychology, was an avid horsewoman and had spent three of the four summers in Jackson as an assistant wrangler at the Lost Creek Dude Ranch.

During the past summer, she had worked as a counselor in the Jackson Hole Day Care Center and was slated to begin a job with a group doing research on child psychology at UCLA. During the summer, she had shared an apartment with another female counselor at the day-care center. Maddy was tall, blonde and, by any standard, attractive, intelligent, and independent.

Maddy's oldest sister was married to an up-and-coming lawyer in Los Angeles. They had two children and lived in a beautiful home in Pacific Palisades. The Hintons' oldest child, Ted, was an investment banker in San Francisco, well on his way to making his own fortune.

In a world fraught with dysfunctional families, the Hintons thanked their lucky stars for their good fortune. They adored their children and were certain that their children adored them. They had been kind and loving parents, respecting their children's privacy and nurturing their independent spirit. They believed that they had guided them with a wise and loving hand, providing them with the wherewithal to find their own path in a world offering far more opportunity than was open to them in their early days. They were generous but not indulgent, sensing that a limitless pocketbook would be ruinous to their children's future. They were certain that their children were well on the way to making successes of their lives.

Maddy, of course, understood how her parents viewed their lives. She was well aware of what they hoped for in terms of their children's futures. She had thought long and hard of how she was going to tell them of her decision, finally deciding that there was no point in subterfuge or vacillation. They simply would have to understand.

Mrs. Hinton sipped her glass of white wine and exchanged glances with her husband who, she knew, was equally disturbed by their daughter's sudden announcement.

"What about your job with the UCLA group?" Mr. Hinton asked. Maddy felt him studying her face.

"I'm not taking it, dad," Maddy said.

"But why?" Mrs. Hinted asked. "It's a fabulous opportunity."

"Yes, it is."

"You know," Mr. Hinton said, "that your mother and I will support you in any endeavor you choose, Maddy."

"I appreciate that, dad."

"I suppose you'll stay on with the day-care center," Mrs. Hinton said.

"I'm not sure."

"Is Dotty staying on?" Mrs. Hinton asked, referring to the girl with whom Maddy shared her apartment.

"No, she's not."

"Will you stay in the apartment, then?" Mr. Hinton asked. "Of course, you're welcome to stay in the house."

"Thank you, dad, but I've made other arrangements."

Again, Mr. And Mrs. Hinton exchanged glances. Maddy could sense the stirring of their anxiety.

"Other arrangements?" Mrs. Hinton asked.

Maddy felt a heightening of trepidation. Her revelation, she knew, would come as a shock. She hadn't prepared them.

"I'm moving in with Luke Prescott," she said, averting her eyes.

"Who?"

"Luke Prescott," Maddy said. "You met him briefly at the Alliance picnic."

"The tall fellow with the drooping mustache?" Mrs. Hinton asked.

"That's him. His mother was a Shoshone."

"A what?"

"A Shoshone Indian. Years ago, they spent summers hunting here."

"Did they?" Mrs. Hinton said. Although they had surrounded themselves with the facade of the Western mythology, they knew little about the history of early Jackson Hole.

"We should really bone up on those early days," Mr. Hinton said, finishing his wine, pouring himself another and topping Mrs. Hinton's glass. Maddy declined, having hardly touched her glass.

In terms of Luke Prescott, Maddy knew she hadn't been forthcoming. Except for that one brief meeting at the Alliance picnic, she hadn't brought Luke home to socialize with her parents. In fact, she had been downright secretive. At the Alliance picnic, he was introduced to them as her "friend", a mere date, a perfectly acceptable temporary relationship with one of the local boys.

They had treated him accordingly. If they had sensed that the relationship was more than that, she suspected that their reaction would have been standoffish and suspicious.

While her parents may have been curious, silent observers, she had always kept her social life to herself. She saw no reason to share confidences with her mother about her love life, nor was her mother overly intrusive. Besides, the Hintons' other children had settled into acceptable patterns. They had no reason to believe that Maddy would do otherwise.

"Are you sure about this, Maddy?" Mrs. Hinton said, trying to mask her concern by sipping deeply of her wine.

"Very much so, Mom."

"It does seem like you're missing out on an opportunity," Mr. Hinton said.

"I've taken that into account, dad."

"What was the boy's name?" Mrs. Hinton asked.

"Luke Prescott. He grew up here in the valley."

"Did he?" Mrs. Hinton said.

"Real nice people, Mom. His father managed the Bear Paw Ranch."

"What does the boy do?" Mr. Hinton asked.

Maddy had no illusions as to where this inquiry was heading.

"He works construction."

"I see."

Mr. and Mrs. Hinton exchanged glances. Maddy had expected that. She knew what was running through their minds.

"I know. It's not exactly a prestigious calling, but he does have a college degree. This is his choice. He wants to stay in the valley."

"And what is your choice, Maddy?" Mrs. Hinton asked.

"I love him, Mom."

"That doesn't answer the question, Maddy," Mr. Hinton interrupted. When he was agitated, a small nerve palpitated in his jaw. It was palpitating now.

"I love Jackson Hole. I like my life here and I want to share it with the man I love."

"I understand that, Maddy. I really do," Mrs. Hinton said. "But are you sure you're taking the long-term view."

"Which is?"

"What your mother means is that sooner or later you'll have to get back to the real world," Mr. Hinton said, finishing his drink and pouring another.

"Oh," Maddy sighed. "And what exactly is the real world?"

"You know what I mean," Mr. Hinton said.

"Of course, she does," Mrs. Hinton rejoined.

"Is this the real world?" Maddy said, her arm sweeping the area of neatly mowed fairways and the landscaping of large well-tended houses.

"It's real to us, Maddy," Mr. Hinton said. "And it was real to you in the summers we've spent here." He searched her face and cleared his throat. "All we're asking, Maddy, is that you consider the consequences."

He lifted the wine bottle and noted that it was empty.

"You mean the consequences of living down, on less money, of being part of the blue-collar crowd, of associating with the lessers, the working stiffs." Maddy's anger mounted as she reacted to Mr. Hinton's remark.

"They're just living together, Charles," Mrs. Hinton said. "She hasn't announced their engagement."

"One thing leads to another," Mr. Hinton muttered, sipping his drink and shaking his head. He held the empty wine bottle by the neck and stood up.

"Besides," Mrs. Hinton said, her cautionary tone obvious, "doing construction may be just an interim situation." She turned to her daughter. "Young people do odd jobs, like waiting on tables, until they move on to better things."

"What does this boy have in mind?" Mr. Hinton said, turning to his daughter.

"At the moment, he's perfectly content with his job. It gives him time to do the things he loves the most."

Maddy knew, of course, that her parents' idea of the so-called good life was totally different than Luke's . . . and hers. She paused for a long moment, trying to assemble her thoughts. She truly wanted them to understand.

"He loves the valley, its hiking trails, the beauty of its mountain ranges, the wildflowers in summer, downhill skiing and snowmobiling in winter. He loves hunting and horseback riding and won't eat any meat but game meat, which is the main reason he hunts. He likes to fish like you, dad. He writes poetry and loves to read. He likes the radical change of seasons, loves the cold of winter and the warmth of summer and the lovely displays of autumn. He feels free only when he breathes the air of

Jackson Hole. He loves his friends here, his family and his dogs. He knows he will wither away outside of the valley, especially in the big cities, where financial success and celebrity counts for everything. He knows he will have to live more frugally in the valley, but he doesn't think of that as a sacrifice. And most important, he loves me, and the fact is he wants to spend the rest of his life with me."

She sensed that her parents were looking at her with astonishment and, despite their outward pride in the way she had expressed herself, with anxiety. For a long time, there was silence. Mr. Hinton had been standing. Suddenly he looked at the empty bottle he was holding, then muttered something about getting another, and went into the house.

"I think I upset dad," Maddy said.

"Well, your decision has come as a shock."

"I know. And I'm sorry for that. But we've always been forthright, Mom. It's my life and my decision."

"Yes, it is," Mrs. Hinton said, finishing her wine and putting the wine glass on the table beside her. "Of course, we are your parents."

"Certainly, Mom, I mean no disrespect."

"Did I suggest that you were disrespectful?" Mrs. Hinton said testily.

"No, you didn't," Maddy said, slipping into a long silence. Mother and daughter sat quietly until Mr. Hinton returned. He had uncorked the bottle and poured wine into Mrs. Hinton's empty glass, then into his own, which he lifted to his lips and took a deep draw, nodding his approval.

"Maddy, darling," he began. Obviously, he had been thinking about how he should react during his trek to get the fresh bottle of wine.

"You don't know what it means to struggle economically in this country. It's no fun doing without. We worked hard so that you and your brother and sister would have a better life without the anxiety of financial hardship. Believe me, when you have children of your own, you'll understand. I'm not saying this boy is not the right one for you. All I'm saying is that you should think long and hard about this decision."

"That's all your father is saying, Maddy," Mrs. Hinton said. "Think before you jump."

She knew the shorthand of their remarks. It would not be the first time that a girl of means had fallen in love with a so-called townie. For her parents, this was another culture and despite their background, they had slotted themselves into a class beyond their humble beginnings and now were as much a part of it as if they had inherited their fortune.

The truth was that she did not relate to the country-club life and their illusion of privilege. They had climbed the only mountain in their field of vision at the time and they felt victorious. What they did not understand was that the battleground had shifted.

She had come to realize that her vision of the good life was more like Luke's, not simply because she loved him, but because he had shown her that there were other ways to look at the world. The acquisition of material wealth was not the only path to life's harvest. The balance had shifted. Quality of life was more a priority than an overabundance of possessions. The natural world, simplicity, esthetics, ecological concerns, a sense of freedom, had more weight with her than accumulated wealth.

Mr. and Mrs. Hinton were silent for a long time, but their inaudibility was not without voice or expression. Her parents' silence told her a great deal. She knew they loved her, but their disappointment in her decision was obvious. She

had expected that, and it had been her choice not to expose Luke to their attitude, which, despite their denial, would
be just as obvious to him.

"I wish you would just think it through," Mr. Hinton said.
Maddy noted that his face was slightly flushed, a sure sign
of his drinking more than he should. The idea was reaf-
firmed when he finished his drink and repoured another.

"I have, dad."

"I guess it comes under the heading of sowing wild oats,"
Mr. Hinton said.

"I wish," Mrs. Hinton said, holding out her glass. Mr.
Hinton poured.

"It's not exactly a shrewd move, Maddy," Mr. Hinton said.
Maddy noted that his speech had thickened.

"Shrewd? Is that your criteria for decision-making, dad?"
She immediately regretted her words, hating the way this
conversation was going.

"All right then, Maddy. How about dumb?"

Mrs. Hinton remained silent, looking into her wine
glass, knowing that an unavoidable confrontation was
on its way.

"Dumb? Being in love is dumb? Wanting to stay here
with the man I love is dumb? Wanting to live here forever is
dumb?"

"Forever, is it?" Mr. Hinton said, his face reddening. "Yes,
it's dumb to throw away your life. Where is the future in
this decision?"

"We're taking it one day at a time," Maddy said.

"Take one wrong turn and it'll be tough getting back,"
Mr. Hinton said. "My advice is turn back. You're going in
the wrong direction. You can't contemplate the consequences when you make an emotional decision. There's no
prospects here. You know it and I know it."

"Maybe we can help him get a good job with a good future," Mrs. Hinton began, then stopped abruptly.

Maddy shook her head in despair.

"You just don't get it, either of you. This is our choice. A good future for us means living here. We don't measure our success the way you do."

"You will," Mr. Hinton said, pouring himself another drink. "Try being a have-not for a couple of years. See what love will do for you then. Get yourself a couple of kids, you'll see what I mean. You're stepping down, Maddy. That's what you're doing, stepping down. While your brother and sister will be moving up, you'll be stepping down. Don't tell us we don't get it. You'll wind up different than them and different from us."

"How different, dad? Kids with Indian blood? Is that it?".

"Don't be ridiculous, Maddy," Mrs. Hinton said. "You know us better than that."

"I wouldn't foreclose on that, either," Mr. Hinton muttered.

"That's going too far, Ken," Mrs. Hinton said, her nostrils dilating. She, too, appeared to be slightly tipsy.

"Not far enough. In my day, a father stood for something. His children respected the wisdom of his experience. Not so today. Parents are irrelevant today." He turned to Maddy. "You think your father is an irrelevant idiot, a snobbish bigoted son-of-a-bitch, don't you, Maddy? How do I explain to you that you're walking down the wrong path? You think when things turn sour, we'll bail you out. Forget it. No way. Why, I wouldn't want to injure your boy's pride by deigning to offer him help."

"You got that right, dad. He wouldn't take it. Neither would I."

"Sorry. I won't give you the opportunity."

Mr. Hinton upended his glass and poured again to refill it.

"I always thought you were the smartest of the three," Mr. Hinton said. "Now I see you're just another damned fool." He shook his head and took a deep sip. "Hot pants," he mumbled. "It's all about hot pants."

"You're going over the edge, Ken," Mrs. Hinton admonished with rising anxiety.

"Over the edge, is it? I've been a damned good dad and I've got a right to express myself, express how distant her point of view was from her parent's aspirations for her."

"It's our fault, Ken," Mrs. Hinton said. Although she had had much wine, she showed no signs of being out of control. "We encouraged this side of her. We provided her with the opportunity to make such a decision. She never had to worry about economic hardship. Her mind was free to make these philosophical choices."

"Wait until the going gets rough," Mr. Hinton muttered.

"We'll just have to take our chances, dad," Maddy said, hoping her tone would not seem sarcastic. She had handled this badly, she decided, wondering if it would have been better not to be so forthcoming. To her parents, she was entering an alien world, a place they had either forgotten or denied had existed.

"Yes, you will," Mr. Hinton said. He seemed to have calmed, but he looked tired and suddenly old. She realized that she had disappointed him.

"I'm sorry, dad," she said. She wanted to move forward and embrace him, but glancing at her mother and sensing her concern, she decided against it. She stood up.

"I'll be fine," she said, addressing both of them.

Mrs. Hinton nodded, but her father didn't look at her. Understanding their concern did not make it any easier for her.

"Will you stay for dinner?" Mrs. Hinton asked.

"Not tonight, Mom. I promised Luke. . . ." She broke off suddenly and swallowed any further explanation.

"I understand," Mrs. Hinton said, looking briefly at her husband, who had averted his eyes. She finished the wine in her glass.

"Give him our best, Maddy," she said.

Maddy nodded and stood up, then turned and walked away.